GOD KING

GOD KING

JOANNE WILLIAMSON

BETHLEHEM BOOKS • IGNATIUS PRESS
BATHGATE, N.D.   SAN FRANCISCO

Text © 2002 Joanne Williamson
Introduction © 2002 Daria Sockey
Special features © 2002 Bethlehem Books

Cover design by Davin Carlson
Front cover illustration © 2002 Dominick Saponaro
Back cover and inside illustrations by Roseanne Sharpe

First printing, April 2002

ISBN 978-1-883937-73-7
Library of Congress control number: 2002102848

Bethlehem Books • Ignatius Press
10194 Garfield Street South
Bathgate, ND 58216
www.bethlehembooks.com

Printed in the United States on acid free paper

Manufactured by Thomson-Shore, Dexter, MI (USA); RMA590DS991, August 2013

Contents

	Introduction	IX
	Prologue	XIX
1.	Crocodile!	1
2.	Death of a God	8
3.	Shabataka	14
4.	The Journey	31
5.	God and Goddess	41
6.	Gathering Clouds	46
7.	Embutah!	51
8.	The Smile on the High Priest's Face	60
9.	Nightmare	66
10.	The House of Talos	77
11.	Physician	84
12.	Shabataka, My Brother	89
13.	Flight From Thebes	94
14.	No Ships to the East	104
15.	Shabataka in the Night	116
16.	The Sea and the Smoke	124
17.	Rab Shaka	128
18.	The Tabernacle	135
19.	"Don't Let Them See You Cry"	139
20.	"Pharaoh, King of Egypt"	147
21.	The Spring and the Tunnel	158
22.	The Mad King	168
23.	"He Will not Come Into the City"	178
24.	The Man With the Scar	186
25.	The Confrontation	195
26.	The Return of a King	202
	Author's Note	

Introduction

THE PERIOD of Egyptian history (around 710-702 B.C.) depicted in *God King* is pretty obscure to the average person. We tend to study "Ancient Civilizations" during the mid-to-late elementary years. The typical unit on Egypt emphasizes the time between the unification of the Two Kingdoms through the Age of the Pyramids (The Old Kingdom: about 3100-2600); then the heights of Egypt's political power during the reign of Thutmose III (1504-1450 B.C.*). Akhenaton (1379-1362 B.C.) and his interesting but failed attempt to impose monotheism on Egypt is studied next. His successor, the very weak Pharaoh Tutankamon, is only mentioned in conjunction with the modern recovery of his tomb and its spectacular treasure.

From around 1100 B.C. Egypt's national power degenerated, due to the kinds of cutthroat political power struggles that seem inevitable to every large empire. So it is easy to see why this is the place where many teachers and textbooks give a brief summary of Egypt's decline, and move on to the more interesting things happening in Ancient Greece. Egypt

---

* Egyptian dates in this introduction are from the *Encyclopedia Britannica*

doesn't reappear on the scene until Alexander the Great's conquest of it in 332 B.C.

God King fills in this gap. What is even more valuable, it helps us connect various ancient cultures in our minds—Kush, Egypt, Assyria and Judea. Too often, we study one culture or country in isolation from others. A novel such as *God King* breaks through this narrow focus and builds a more unified sense of ancient history, and along with it, a sense of the historicity of Sacred Scripture.

As our story opens, Egypt has been under the rule of Kush (located in what is at present northern Sudan) for several generations. The New Kingdom with its long series of dynasties had collapsed. First Libyan princes from the west, and now Kushite leaders from the south had each succeeded for a time in imposing their own dynastic rule on Egypt. But as the rapidly expanding Assyria in the north absorbs one nation after another, Egypt is very interested in maintaining a buffer zone between itself and these latest invaders. Thus it is supporting Palestine and Phoenicia in their doomed efforts to ward off the Assyrian threat. Now the king of Judea hopes for that same support.

Since the death of King Solomon around 922 B.C., Israel had been divided into two kingdoms, Israel in the North, and Judea in the South. Both kingdoms had been weakened by conflict with one another. Worse still, as the Old Testament Scriptures relate, God's chosen people in both kingdoms had largely turned to idolatry, often with the encouragement of their kings. The Northern Kingdom had fallen to Assyria in 721—less than a generation before the events of our story. Over her history, only eight of Judea's twenty kings worshipped the true God, and even these did little or nothing to abolish idol worship among the people. It was during these centuries that great prophets such as Isaiah, Jeremiah, and Joel called upon the people and their rulers to reform. Hezekiah, the King of Judea whom we meet in this book, was one of those few whose faith in God was rewarded. His kingdom, although much reduced, was not annihilated by the Assyrians. This story speculates about the persons and events through which God arranged this.

Well-researched, well written fiction like *God King* opens our mind and imagination to the past. We learn about a people's everyday customs—how they ate, dressed, conducted business, worshipped, etc. We pay better attention to such a presentation of customs than we would by simply reading about it in a textbook, for now we care about the characters who use these customs. It all comes alive. Because these fictional characters are given real personalities, we see them reacting to various situations with anger, humor, fear, embarrassment, or affection—just as we would. We can gaze across enormous chasms of time and culture and look into the eyes of friends. Sons of Adam and Daughters of Eve. Human nature, for better or worse, hasn't changed. This is one of history's greatest lessons.

Notes to the Home Educator

Integrating *God King* into your curriculum is as simple as reading it aloud in the evening, a chapter or two per night. Later on, show your children where this story takes place on a timeline (around 710-702 B.C.), in comparison to other events you have studied in Egyptian, Greek, Roman, or Bible history. Read the biblical passages mentioned in the author's afterword. Compare a map of ancient Egypt and its surroundings with a modern globe. Locate Somalia, Ethiopia, Sudan (where ancient Nubia and Kush were located) and Iraq (Assyria). Look at a map of biblical Palestine and locate the kingdoms of Judah and Samaria.

Fans of the classical or Charlotte Mason method will want to have the children re-tell sections of the story after it is read to them. This may be done orally or in writing, depending on the child's abilities or the homeschool's time constraints. Another approach is not so much to re-tell the story in detail as to summarize each chapter, trying to determine the main point or action that occurred. Although some reluctant student writers need to be encouraged to give detailed descriptions, others have the tendency to cover sheets of paper with needless and repetitive detail. This latter group must learn to reflect, and then to determine what is the essence of the story they have heard. Students like this may be challenged to tell or write in a single sentence the most important event of each chapter.

Depending on your student's age or interest, look up several sources that deal with this period of Egyptian history, and see what is said about Taharka and Shabataka. You will find that they conflict with this book (again, see Author's Note) and probably with one another. Little is known about this time, and scholars have to guess from the small amount of information and legends that exist. Differing viewpoints often turn on the author's recognition or lack of recognition of the Bible as a source of historical information (yet Bible scholars also may differ). If archaeology fascinates your student, you may wish to go to the library to find books and magazines which tell about discoveries in the Middle East. Many of them present facts that strengthen our knowledge of the historical reliability of Scripture.

God King may also be studied as literature. It is a historical novel. Although at its core is a real event, much of the story, in its small events, minor characters, and indeed the personalities of its major characters, is invented. You may wish to compare it in discussion with your student to other historical novels he has enjoyed. Some of these propose to shed light on a real event or person; others dwell mainly on a fictional subplot, with the historical event merely as background. A comparison essay along these lines on two historical novels may be a worthwhile project for an older student.

If your child excels in creative writing, *God King* may inspire him to try his own hand at historical fiction. Find some other event and person in history about whom only a few bare facts are known. Have fun brainstorming possible situations that lead up to the event. What was this person's childhood like? Did he or she, like Taharka, wish at times to escape his role in life and be someone else? Were there any particular strengths or flaws in his personality that affected his future? Who were his best friends in times of trouble? Would you like to work an animal (like Taharka's donkey) into the story? One word of caution. Do not try to do ALL of the above-mentioned activities. A mother's runaway enthusiasm may become a student's overkill. Select one or two activities that seem to fit with your child's abilities. The main event should always be parent and child enjoying a wonderful, memorable story together.

Daria Sockey

SOME OTHER HISTORICAL FICTION RELATED TO EGYPTIAN HISTORY

Shadow Hawk, Andre Norton. Nubia, 1570 B.C.: end of rule of Hyksos and dawn of the 18th dynasty.

Mara, Daughter of the Nile, Eloise Jarvis McGraw. Time of Hatshepsut and Thutmose III around 1480 B.C.

Scarab for Luck, Enid La Monte Meadowcroft. Time of Amenhotep II, son of Thutmose III, 1450-1425 B.C.

The Lost Queen of Egypt, Lucille Morrison. Time of Akhenaton and Tutankhamon, 1350 B.C.

A Camel for a Throne, Eloise Lownsbery. Time of Pharoah Amenemhet, founder of 12th Dynasty of Middle Kingdom, about 2000 B.C.

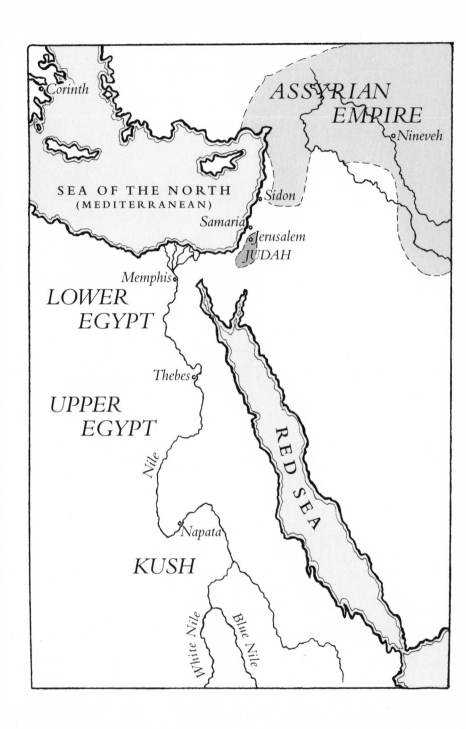

701 B.C.

Be strong and of good courage. Do not be afraid or dismayed before the king of Assyria and all the horde that is with him; for there is one greater with us than with him.

Hezekiah, King of Judah
Bible, II Chronicles 32:7

In the days of Assyria's might even Egypt feared her aggressions. Egypt was then ruled by Kushite princes, around whom one of them, Taharka, this story unfolds.

Prologue

IT WAS CHILDREN'S nap time in the women's quarters, but the boy and the girl in the garden were not asleep.

"Hold him still," said the boy.

The girl held hard to the injured lamb while the boy bound splints to the broken leg, as they had taught him at scribe school.

"Where did you find him?" he asked her.

"In the main kitchen. I was stealing a honey cake."

The boy laughed. "And you came out with this instead?"

"They were going to cook him. Well, they won't cook him now."

He laughed again, patted the animal and watched it hobble off.

"You're good at this," said the girl. "Just like a doctor."

"That's what I would like to be. That, or maybe a soldier. They say I'm good with the staff and the spear, and it would get me out of here." They gazed around at the high walls hemming them into the garden with the lotus pool.

"I'd be anything, to get out of here. Except," the

girl looked suddenly into his eyes. "Except that I wouldn't see you again."

After a moment he looked away. He caught a glimpse of a tall, handsome youth crossing the garden, followed respectfully by two priests. The girl saw him too.

"At least," she said, "I'd never have to see *him* again."

"You'd better get used to him," said the younger boy, soberly. "Someday—"

"Never," said the girl. She rose. "They're calling me. I'll have to go now." She walked slowly toward the door of the Great House where the head nurse awaited her, frowning angrily.

The boy stared up at the high sandstone walls. A prison, he thought. It's like a prison. Except that sometimes they let him out. Like tomorrow. The hunt. He brightened a little at the thought of tomorrow.

He glanced toward where the handsome youth had disappeared around a corner.

At least, he thought, I'll never have to be king.

𑈴 1 𑈵

Crocodile!

"GET BACK in the boat, Lord Taharka! Back!
You must be ready when he comes!"

The boy Taharka stood ankle deep in the thick black mud of the great river. It was hot, hot, hot. Not far away, across the lush green banks, the sun shimmered on sand and rock. The boy's skin, black as the rocks on the bank of the Nile, was protected by a loose white cloth that beat back the wicked rays. Already it was soaked with sweat.

"He's slow. He's lazy," said the boy, though his heart was beating very fast.

"Don't count on it. He can move like the rapids downstream, and you won't hear a sound."

For the first time in his twelve years, Taharka had been brought out on a crocodile hunt. The crocodile was sacred to Sebek, the crocodile god, of course, but that was all right for Taharka was a prince. Not a very important prince, but a prince, one of the many sons of Shabaka, king of Kush, who ruled as a god in the Kushite city of Napata.

He had no quarrel with Sebek (he had been taught that all the gods were his cousins) and was not really looking forward to the killing. But Embutah had said it was a lesson—something that must be learned.

"Don't play games," said Embutah grimly. "This isn't the day for it."

Embutah was his uncle, once a slave, now a high captain in the army. Taharka had always followed his orders without question, so now, heat or no heat, he got back in the boat. He leaned back to gaze at the shimmering blue sky, at the water birds passing overhead. A flock of storks beat by, up river from the great sea of the north, so far away that he did not believe it really existed, though his own grandfather had once seen it. He bowed his head in respect as the sacred ibis skimmed majestically by.

"Look!" said Embutah.

Taharka's heart jumped, for he thought that the crocodile had come. But it was the kingfisher, hovering still as death above them. It dove as he watched, plummeting down like a rock from the sky. The three of them—Taharka, Embutah and Net the boatman—watched spellbound, as if it had been the first time they had seen it.

So they did not realize that the crocodile was really there.

He had come swiftly, as Embutah had warned, only his dark green back showing above the water. He was very hungry and very silent and the first they knew of his presence was the shock to the boat as he struck it with his tremendous tail.

And then the scream. A heart chilling scream, despairing and wild.

Net, the boatman, had fallen into the water.

Taharka had once seen a condemned criminal thrown to the crocodile. He had often dreamt of it. But this was real. This was Net. There was only one thing to do.

He scrambled to the spot from which Net had fallen, seizing the spear with its iron head. Embutah was shouting at him.

"No, Lord, no! Let him go! Get back!"

Sebek was already upon the boatman. Those terrible teeth were closing on his arm. Taharka struck the beast with the spear and, at the same time, saw the water redden with blood—Net's or the crocodile's, he didn't know which. But the flat head was driven aside. And suddenly Sebek had turned on him, the great jaws opened wide as in his dreams, ready to seize and crush him and drag him down.

Something struck him and threw him flat. The jaws had snapped shut, but on the empty air. Embutah was leaning over the side, his powerful hands clamped around the ugly snout, squeezing it shut.

"The spear! The spear! Remember what I taught you!"

His great muscles were trembling. The sweat was pouring down his arms.

Suddenly Taharka was very calm. He grasped the spear, positioning his hands just as Embutah had shown him. He fixed his eyes on the thrashing back of the beast, on the spot where the spear must enter, at the base of the ugly head.

He drove down the spear.

The waters churned. There was a great cry from Embutah, thrown back into the bottom of the boat. Then the waters were dyed red as Taharka had never imagined, and began to grow still.

They dragged the boatman over the side. Blood was spurting from an ugly wound in his arm where the beast's teeth had grazed him. He was trembling with pain and shock.

Taharka could see that the man might bleed to death. He knew a little of what must be done. All the children of the god were instructed in the sacred medicine at their scribe school—the formulas, the prescriptions, the magic spells. The bleeding must be stopped with a tight binding above the wound.

"I can stop the bleeding," Taharka said.

"How? We have no cloth," said Embutah.

Without thinking, Taharka tore off the fine cotton cloth—the sacred cloth, so it was said—that shielded him from the sun. He looked defiantly at Embutah. Embutah was silent. Taharka hesitated, holding it out to the aging warrior, for Embutah had stanched the blood of many battle wounds.

Embutah shook his head.

"Try your skill," he said. "You've come this far. Finish it."

Taharka gritted his teeth. He was frightened. The man's life might depend on what he did. He grasped the wounded arm, feeling for the spot where the terrible spurting must be stopped.

And suddenly he was no longer afraid. He could do it. Blood was life, but after all it was only blood, and if you stopped the leak it couldn't get out.

It must be tight enough. He needed something to twist with. He broke off a stalk of reed. He knotted the cloth in place.

The man lay in the boat, still shaking and moaning. Now that it was over, Taharka found that he was shaking too. But somehow he had never felt better in his life.

Embutah examined the dressing.

"It will hold. It wasn't as bad as I thought."

They were no longer alone. Several of the small reed boats had pulled up close, drawn by the shouts and the cries. Men with nets and wooden spears, hunting for water fowl. They stared at the boy with the emblems of the royal clan of Napata on his thin breast. They whispered together. Embutah pointed one of them out.

"You." He nodded toward the injured boatman. "Take his place."

The fowler, without question, scrambled over the side.

"Away!" Embutah shouted at the others. "What are you looking at? How dare you lift your eyes to a son of the god?"

As they pulled away, Taharka heard one of them mutter, "A son of the god! He has broken the tabu. He has laid hands on a slave. He has bound his wound with the sacred cloth."

Under the burning sun, Taharka felt suddenly cold. The tabu. The law. His flesh was not mortal flesh, he had been taught. His very clothing must not be defiled. He had forgotten about that. What would they do to him when they found out?

But he knew that, even if there had been time to think, he would have done the same.

"I had to do it," he said to Embutah.

"I know. And, you being you, I couldn't have stopped you. Hold your head up and be ready for punishment if it comes. Don't think about it now."

And, on the way back to the city, he tried not to think about it, tried to think about the approach to Napata, which he loved, with its great temple and towering tombs. The air had already begun to hum with voices. The scattered huts along the river bank thickened into clusters stretching as far as he could see.

After a while they came to a quay, and the fowler moored the boat. A chariot was waiting, the driver standing patiently beside it. Behind him stood another man with the solemn, self-important air of an official. But Taharka thought that he looked anxious, even a little frightened.

He waited while Embutah ordered a longshore-man to take the injured boatman to one of the huts. Then he spoke.

"The Lord Taharka is commanded to appear at once in the great hall of the god."

For a moment Taharka couldn't move. Had they found out about the sacred cloth already? But the man spoke again.

"All the children of the Great House are sum-moned. The god is dying."

❧ 2 ❧

Death of a God

TAHARKA thought he could count on his fingers the number of times he had seen his father, though he had sometimes felt his eyes upon him, heard something almost like a chuckle as the awesome figure passed him in its gold-washed litter, borne on the backs of four strong men.

The god had many wives and a great many children. Some were important because their mothers were princesses. Taharka's mother was not; though, of course, the priests had made her one when the god had chosen her. She was just a girl who had been brought with other slaves and a cargo of gold up from the far off Zambesi River. She had died some years before, and Embutah, her brother, was all that Taharka had left of her.

So Taharka was not one of the important children of the god. But they all played together and learned together in the women's quarters—learned reading and writing, languages and dancing, magic and healing and the many laws and tabus of Kush—and, above all, the lore of the gods, their cousins.

Today, Taharka was not taken back to the house of the women. Just as he was, looking like a boatman's boy, he was brought into the god's great chamber to see his father die. The sweat on his face was cold now as he joined the throng of children—brothers, sisters, cousins of all degrees—some of them shivering with fear, some giggling softly in nervous excitement.

His cousin, Shepnuset, was there. Bad little Shepnuset, who had stolen a lamb from the kitchen. They had been keeping a close watch on her since the day another cousin, whose mind had not grown with his body, had reached out smiling to touch a poisonous asp. Shepnuset, attacking the creature with a stick, had almost gotten herself killed. That would have been a disaster, for Shepnuset was the niece and destined heir of Taharka's great aunt, the high priestess of Amon, who ruled as the god's deputy for Egypt in far off Thebes. She would one day be almost more sacred than the king himself.

Taharka liked to look at her. Even today he could not help looking at her, though the other children whispered that she was really not that pretty. It was on the day of the killing of the asp that he had decided that marriage might not be so bad after all. Of course there was no question of his marrying Shepnuset. She was destined for his half-brother Shabataka. That, he thought, was as it should be.

Shabataka. Sixteen years old, tall, strong, grave and handsome. After today, the god. There was no doubt about that. The priests had prepared for it for years. Only Shabataka could really be said to know his father. Only Shabataka was allowed to slip into his presence unannounced. Only Shabataka could stand at his side, listening and learning while the Lord of Kush gave audience. Taharka's reverence for his older brother was second only to his reverence for the god himself. What must Shabataka be feeling now? he wondered. Grief, certainly.

The god himself was not seated on the golden stool as Taharka had always seen him before. His cedarwood couch had been carried into the great hall. He lay upon it, propped up on cushions, his breath faint, his clouded eyes wandering over the faces of the priests and magicians and captains and the many wives and children.

"Why are they here?" he whispered. "Must I give a judgment?"

The priest of Sebek the crocodile was on his knees beside the couch.

"Yes, a judgment, Great God. The time has come. You must take the wand of succession in your hand. You must declare your choice."

"My sons," said the god Shabaka. "Bring them to me. Pi-Ankhi—Shabataka—Kashta—Taharka—"

"Taharka, no!" said the crocodile priest. He raised his head from the ground and spoke so all could hear him. "The Lord Taharka has broken a tabu. He has touched the flesh of a slave. His godhood is sullied. We will pass judgment on him later."

Taharka could not have moved. They knew! How had they known so quickly? It didn't matter. They knew.

The god was speaking. His voice was stronger.

"*We* will pass judgment? *I* am the god on earth. *I* will pass judgment. Taharka my son, seed of my father Pi-Ankhi, seed of my father Kashta the king, come to me."

On his knees and elbows Taharka crawled the length of the stone floor to his father's couch. The god's voice was weaker now.

"Why have you done this thing?"

Taharka raised his head.

"The man would have died," he whispered.

Though it was forbidden to look into the god's eyes, Taharka knew that, through the mist of weakness and pain, they were as hard as the black rock of the holy mountain. In terror, he searched for words that the god would understand.

Suddenly he found them. He straightened on his knees and his voice rang out as firmly as the voice of the priest of Sebek.

"The man belonged to the God. Everything belongs to the God—the water of the river, the grain in the fields, the laborers and priests and chieftains of the land. I, too, am the slave of the God. I must preserve what belongs to you, Great God Shabaka."

The great god Shabaka fell back upon his cushion.

A groan of dismay ran around the great chamber. If the dying man had used up his strength on this trifling matter, what would become of the succession? Would the land be left without a god on earth to bring the rising of the sun and the flooding of the river and the growth of the grain?

But the god had raised a trembling hand. The priest of the sun in Napata hastened to place within it the wand of gold, the magic wand of succession, the scepter of the god. The wand wavered a moment, then fell. Its tip pointed toward the boy kneeling beside the couch.

There was a long moment's silence. The figure on the couch did not move. At last the priest of the sun broke the silence.

"The Great God," he said, "has become one with his father. See the wand of succession. It has declared his choice."

The priests, the warriors, the many wives and children, fell upon their knees, their foreheads pressed to the cold floor of the chamber. Taharka heard again the voice of the sun priest.

"Taharka, child of the god, rise."

He was trembling. What did it mean? What had happened? Was he to be punished now?

His hands were being crossed upon his breast. Something cold and smooth was being pressed into them.

It was the golden wand of the god.

"Take possession of the land, Taharka, soul of the

hawk, beautiful child of Ra, son of the sun, bringer of the Nile, Lord of Kush, Great God of Napata and Meroe, and Pharaoh of Egypt."

Taharka had become a god.

He had also received his punishment.

❧ 3 ❧

Shabataka

THE PUNISHMENT was this: Taharka, the Kushite boy, was now all those things that the priest of the sun had called him. He was king of a land that stretched from the mouth of the Nile on the Northern Sea—some day to be known as the Mediterranean Sea—to the southern border of Kush.

He was immensely rich. He owned copper mines in the Sinai desert, gold mines in the highlands of Ethiopia and the jungles of Zimbabwe. He owned every inch of farmland and forest land, every wild beast and every goat and sheep and cow. He also owned every man, woman and child, and every fruit of their labor, for he was the god on earth.

As the god, he had many duties. He must be up before the sun and in his golden chair, carried by four porters around the walls of the Great House— for if he were not there, the sun would not rise at all! He must be on his golden stool before the sun was high to receive the gifts of foreign princes and tribal chiefs (which were then shut away somewhere

14

where he would probably never see them again.) There were the judgments, and this he hated most of all, for the sun priest had already decided them, and cruel as they might be, he was expected to pronounce them. After a while, he let the sun priest make the pronouncements himself. The sun priest raised no objections.

And there were the tabus. Now that he was the god, so many things were forbidden him. He could eat no meat but the flesh of a calf or a goose, and only flat bread made without yeast. Only at certain hours of the day, or at festivals, was he allowed outside the walls of the Great House; and then his head must be covered by the double crown and his feet must not touch the ground. The day of the crocodile hunt, the sun on his skin, the mud on his feet, began to seem like a wonderful, impossible dream.

Taharka had become a prisoner, a prisoner who must not even dream of escape. For if any of the tabus were broken, he knew that disaster would come upon the people. The sun would not rise in the morning, the river would not rise, and all the land would dry up and wither away.

He was very lonely. Those who spoke to him must kneel, their faces to the ground, for it was believed that the sight of Pharaoh's radiant face would strike a man blind. For that matter, not many people were allowed to speak to him at all.

Of course, there was Shepnuset.

Shepnuset, the untouchable Shepnuset—little Prin-

cess High-and-Mighty, the other children sneered—
was now his betrothed wife. This was the law. If the
wand had pointed to a beggar boy, that boy would
have become the god. And he would have had to
marry Shepnuset.

This, at first, had seemed the strangest thing of
all. At first he had hardly dared speak to her. What
would he say?

The first thing she said to him was: "Are you
hungry?"

And, forgetting his shyness for a moment, he answered her:

"I'm starving!"

She dumped a handful of dates into his lap. He
wasn't sure if he was supposed to eat them, but he
did.

From then on, talking to Shepnuset was no more
a problem than it had ever been. Shepnuset loved to
talk—about her lessons and how to get out of them,
about the tabus and how to get around them, about
food (sometimes he thought he would have starved
to death if it hadn't been for Shepnu!).

Sometimes she talked about the future.

"I'll hate it," she said as they sat together by the
pool in the courtyard. (She had smuggled in some of
the honey cakes made from the unleavened dough—
she had wanted to bring in the forbidden ones, but
Taharka hadn't dared to go that far.)

"Hate what?" said Taharka.

"Everything about it," said Shepnu. "Living in

Egypt. Being shut up all day in that temple in Thebes. I'll be like you then, Hari, only worse. They'll
make me give oracles. You know what that means?"

Taharka didn't answer. She had told him before.
She told him again.

"They'll make me breathe poppy smoke. I'll go
out of my head and say stupid things and they'll say
it's the god Amon talking."

"Well, won't it be?" said Taharka, to annoy her.
He succeeded.

"What a baby! They can make you believe anything."

He laughed. Shepnu looked at him sideways. Her
voice softened.

"Besides. You won't be there."

Taharka's heart quickened a little. He could not
marry Shepnu till he was sixteen, but he often thought
about it—and not just because his name would not
be inscribed as king till that day came. He had decided that Shepnuset really was pretty, whatever the
other children said.

"Your aunt will probably live a long time," he said.
"And even after they take you away, they'll have to
let me visit you." His eyes brightened. "I'll like that.
Down the river to Thebes—Egypt—what a journey!
They say it takes 30 days!"

Shepnuset was always practical.

"They won't let you go till you have chosen your
Companion. Have you done it?"

"Yes. It will be Shabataka." Shabataka, who should

have been the god. Who had listened while his Father gave audiences and pronounced judgments. Who knew all the rituals Taharka was learning so painfully.

Shepnuset looked suddenly troubled. Why? wondered Taharka.

The Companion of the god was closest of all to the king—almost, in fact, his double. In recent years he had come to perform all those things that the priests had decided Pharaoh must not do. He led the armies to the front. And, when Pharaoh must journey to the north, he remained behind to perform all the duties of the god.

Yes, it would be Shabataka, Shabataka, the cleverest and most capable of them all. Shabataka, who had stood so still, his face so unreadable on the day of the great Mistake.

Shabataka, who should have been the god.

About a week after the Mistake, he had come into Taharka's presence, on his feet and smiling right into his brother's face.

"No, no, my brother," Taharka had cried out, afraid for a moment that the handsome youth would be struck blind before his eyes.

"What are you afraid of, Hari?"

"You have broken the tabu!"

"So have you, brother. Have *you* been punished?"

Seeing that Shabataka's eyes were as bright and sharp as ever, Taharka's fears were calmed. He was not, after all, the baby Shepnu had always thought him.

Besides, the gods knew who should be king and who should not.

"I've been punished," he said. "They've put me in a cage."

Shabataka looked around at the sandstone columns and the cedarwood stools and couches inlaid with gold, all the things that belonged to Taharka.

"This is a cage? Being the god is a punishment? All this and, in a little while, to choose all the wives you want and any wife you want? The priests will turn her into a princess for you."

He's thinking of my mother, thought Taharka. Shabataka himself was the son of a real princess—a princess of the proud Somalis in Punt.

But no one, not even Shabataka, would ever make him ashamed of his mother. He did not have to force the royal frown that he leveled at his half-brother.

But Shabataka began to make a habit of coming to the room with the lotus pool. He didn't say much at first, just sat there listening to what Taharka had to say, always watching. It made Taharka a little uncomfortable, as if his brother were listening for something behind his words, something that Taharka himself did not know was there.

But after a while, he seemed to relax, to forget whatever it was he was listening for. Sometimes he almost chuckled.

"No, no, no! You don't obey the sun priest, he obeys you. And when old lady Memnet drops her comb in your presence, you don't go over and pick it up for her."

"She has a bad back. She shouldn't bend over."

"That's the doctor talking. You're not a doctor, brother. You're the god."

For a moment the old shadow darkened his eyes. For some reason, in spite of the heat, Taharka felt a chill.

Shabataka often told him he did not know how to be the god.

"The judgments, for instance. You should decide them, not the sun priest."

"I don't like to judge people. Who knows? There may be reasons for the things they do."

"Yes, you and the vizier. He's as soft as you are. I was taught differently. My—"

He stopped. Taharka knew what he had been about to say. It was strange, but they never seemed to mention their father. Something seemed to hold them back.

But he had begun to take Shabataka's advice. About some things. The sun priest, for instance. There was the day the farmer was sentenced to lose a hand for striking the tax collector.

"No," said Taharka.

There was a buzz of surprise and the sun priest looked annoyed, as if a fly had stung him.

"The judgment has been given, Great God."

"*I* have not given it."

It was as if his father, the god, had spoken, not

little Taharka the son of the Bantu slave girl. For the
first time in his life, he felt the thrill of power.

"The man says he has already paid his tribute. He
says the agent was assessing him double. You haven't
proved he was lying. The case is dismissed."

He closed his eyes, waiting for the roar of protest.
He would not have been surprised if they had simply ignored the interruption. But nothing happened.
The man was hustled out of the hall, never looking
back—he might have thanked me, thought Taharka.
The scribes and officials bowed their heads in sub-
mission. Only a dark glint in the eyes of the sun
priest offered a hint that something different was
happening, that something had gone wrong.

And that evening Shabataka said to him, "That's
not what I meant!"

"You said the judgments should come from me."

Shabataka opened his mouth, then closed it. He
shook his head.

His eyes flickered back to the checkers board. They
had been playing draughts. Shabataka liked to gamble. Shabataka always won. He had won everything
that day—Taharka's gold rings, his ivory-inlaid hounds
and jackals board, his dagger with the iron blade.
Taharka had nothing left to bet.

"The cobra," said Shabataka.

He was smiling. There was something strange
about his smile.

Taharka stared at him. For a moment he thought
he had misunderstood. The cobra? The coiled, gold

cobra worn on the god's brow at ceremonies, the most sacred symbol of his godhood?

Shabataka was watching him, still with that strange smile. You wouldn't dare, his eyes were saying.

"All right," said Taharka. "I'll do it."

For the first time Shabataka's smile slipped. Taharka went a little crazy.

"Why not? I don't want it. If you want it, take it. It was meant for you anyway."

"You mean it," said Shabataka softly. "You'd do it."

"Yes I would," said Taharka. "I want—"

What did he want? To do as he pleased when he pleased to do it, to wrestle again with his brothers and cousins, to—he thought of that day on the river, the man with the gash in his arm, the wonderful feeling of satisfaction as the terrible bleeding stopped. Yes, he would like to learn more about that. He would like to study, he would like to work—

"I don't want to be a prisoner!"

"Be quiet!"

There was a dangerous glitter in the older boy's eyes.

"Listen, Hari. I would have given my *ka*, my soul, to have been chosen that day. Don't talk to me any more of prisons."

"You would give your *ka* never to go boating on the Nile or drive a horse or speak to anyone who isn't crawling like a beetle?"

"Let them try to stop *me* from driving a chariot!

Let them try to stop *me* from *anything*! And," he
added softly, "I would like to see some of them
crawl."

He paused a moment, his eyes looking far off. "I
would let other nations know that there is a God in
Egypt—even the Assyrians would know!"

The Assyrians? Who were the Assyrians?

But then, Shabataka laughed and poked his
brother's shoulder with his fist.

"Don't worry. I'm not the god. You are. I'll teach
you how to be one."

Taharka no longer feared that his radiant face
might blind anyone. He often tried to make Embutah stand or sit in his presence, but his uncle would
no longer do so.

"The forbidden things are the forbidden things,"
he said. "You are the God. I owe you the respect."

With Shabataka's encouragement, Taharka had begun his weapons training again. Embutah knelt beside
him while he ran in place or lifted the weights or
hurled the spear at the wooden target. And sometimes Embutah did spring to his feet to correct him
in his stance or in the grasp of his weapon.

And then, when practice was over and Taharka
sat by the pool, wiping off the sweat, Embutah still
sometimes told him stories.

"Tell me about how we became the lords of
Egypt."

"You can read it for yourself on the great stone when they take you to the temple."

"But I like to hear you tell it."

And Embutah would tell it again. He himself could not read, but he loved the story and had had it repeated till he knew it by heart.

"In the days of Kashta, king of Kush, Egypt our neighbor to the north had fallen on evil days. There *was* no more Egypt! Desert tribes ruled it, piece by piece, and laughed at the gods and sent bands of thieves to rob the tombs of their holy treasures. There was famine, for these barbarians knew nothing about watering the land with the Nile, and all the fields were drying up into desert. So messengers from Thebes came south to Kush and knelt before the Kushite king and swore their allegiance and begged for his help. They set the white crown of the Egyptian southland upon his head and he began to restore their land. But the northland, where the great river spreads out into fingers and flows into the sea, suffered still.

"Then great Kashta died. And one day a courier came to his son Pi-Ankhi, your father's father, on this very roof where you are sitting now. 'Great one,' he said. 'Fearful news! A barbarian chief from the great northern sea has sailed south with many men and horses and is laying waste the villages of Egypt. He has dared to call himself Pharaoh!'

"Your father's father, Pi-Ankhi, sprang to his feet in terrible anger. 'By the hawk and the crocodile, and by the sun whose son I am! The white crown of

Egypt is mine as it was my father's. And now I will utterly destroy this barbarian. I will have the red crown too, the crown of the north. Egypt will be one again, and I will have it all!'

"How the soldiers cheered him, crying, 'It is thy name that gives us strength! Thy bread is in our bellies, thy beer quenches our thirst! It is thy valor that gives us might and there is strength in thy very name!'

"So Pi-Ankhi sailed north in the royal barge, and the river banks on either side were black with soldiers marching. Great Thebes thronged to him, weeping for joy. Into the very strongholds of the north he sailed. The people welcomed him and drove out the pale-skinned barbarian and Egypt was one again. And your father set the double crown—the white and the red—upon his head and surveyed the land as far as the great northern sea, and he wept at the ruin the barbarian had caused. And what angered him the most was that the horses had not been well tended."

Embutah sighed and wiped his forehead from the excitement of the story. Taharka sighed too.

But he was thinking. Something was troubling him.

"Uncle," he said, "was it really Pi-Ankhi the Great who did all that? Not a Companion?"

"By my honor, it was your father's father himself! He chose his son, your father's brother who died later, to share his crown and remain in Napata. I was only a boy, but I remember it well."

Taharka thought about this, balancing the wooden spear. So a Companion could work both ways. He could stay at home and perform the rites while the god put himself in peril, if he chose to do so. And, of course, a real king, a great king like Pi-Ankhi, *would* choose to do so.

He was not sure he liked the idea.

He knew something about war. There were always the desert uprisings and invasions. He and the other royal students had once been taken to a place where wounded soldiers lay, as a lesson in anatomy. He had never forgotten it.

Yes, there had been wars. There would be others. And—

"Uncle," he said, "who are the Assyrians?"

Embutah looked at him sharply.

"So you have heard the name."

He had heard more than just the name that Shabataka had mentioned. Even here in Kush, people whispered about the Assyrians. They always seemed to whisper. A strange and alien people far, far away, lurking in distant mountains on the edge of the world like shadowy beasts of prey in a child's bad dream, reaching out with long, strong arms to grasp and crush all around them.

"The Assyrians are a cloud, nephew," said Embutah. "A far-off cloud."

A cloud. Taharka felt a little relieved. That wasn't so bad. A cloud wasn't real.

"Ambassadors once came here to Napata to ask

your father for help against the Assyrians," said Embutah. "From the kingdom of Israel, way up north, to the east. What with the desert tribes in the west and all that was to be done at home, your father had none to give." He added thoughtfully, "Israel hasn't been heard from since."

That wasn't so good. Israel was a real place. That made the Assyrians seem more real. He thought of the stories he had heard.

"They take people away," he said, and found that he was whispering too. "Just take them away, and they are never heard of again. Shabataka told me that. He was trying to frighten me, but he said he thought it was a good idea. He said he thought they had a lot of good ideas."

"I'm sure he did," said Embutah grimly.

"They take them away, all of them, with ropes around their necks. Like—like what happened to you and my mother."

There was a silence. Embutah had often told him the story of what had happened to him and his little sister, Taharka's mother. It was a terrible story—how the soldiers of Kush had come to the market town on the far-off Zambesi river—how he, a young man and his sister, a child, had been loaded onto one of their great sailing boats to be brought back up the coast to Punt and inland to Kush—he to be sold into the army, she to be sold into a wealthy family that would one day be brought to the attention of the god—

But that story had had a happy ending. He wondered how many happy endings there were in the
stories of people who had anything to do with the
Assyrians.

Shepnuset's aunt, the high priestess in Thebes,
died sooner than was expected. She had to be replaced at once. Taharka, stunned, was faced with
the loss of his closest, almost his only companion.
And something more, though he wasn't quite sure
what it was. Lately it had frightened him a little.
But not since his mother's death had he felt such a
sense of loss.

Shepnuset, as always, tried to be brave.

"After all, Hari, this means that you really will
come to Thebes when you are sixteen. You'll have to!
And you'll make the great journey, see all the sights.
Only four years, Hari."

She began to cry again, and Taharka said, "Four
years!"

He couldn't see into that unimaginable future.

Another blow followed soon. It was Embutah's
fault. Shabataka came to the room with the lotus
pool while Taharka was exercising with his uncle.
He came in as usual, boldly on his feet. And Embutah forgot himself in his anger, ordering the haughty
son of the god to his knees as if he had been an
insolent servant.

Shabataka's eyes flashed lightning.

"Slave, filth from the jungle, you backwoods Bantu! I am forbidden to soil my hands with you, but I will send a slave with your punishment!"

"Brother!" For the first time in his life, Taharka felt a terrible anger. "Embutah is the uncle of the God. No one but the God will dare punish him! Do you think that *you* are the god?"

For a moment the lightning flashed upon Taharka himself. It was as if Shabataka were indeed the god, that the terrible light would blind the pretender. Then the light was hidden. Shabataka fell to his knees and crawled backward from the room with the lotus pool.

Now Taharka's anger turned upon Embutah.

"Why did you do that? Shepnu is gone. Shabataka is all I have left. Now I no longer have *him*!"

"Great God, Great God, my little nephew!" cried Embutah, his own head carefully bent. "If it were right and safe to face the God as an equal, would I not have done it long ago?"

"Safe for whom? Has Shabataka been blinded? Have *you* been blinded?"

"Safe for *you*, my Lord God, safe for *you*!" The words broke from Embutah as if against his will. "The Great God is the great god *because* he is the great god. What will become of him when he is no longer feared?"

Taharka slumped on the stone seat.

"This child of the god, Shabataka," said Embutah

softly, "this son of a Somali princess, he does not fear anything. Make him fear you, Nephew. Make him fear you, if—"

"If what?"

"If you want to go on being alive!"

For a moment, Taharka remembered the shadow in Shabataka's eyes. He put it out of his mind. Shabataka was his brother.

Shabataka no longer came to the room with the lotus pool; and whenever Taharka passed him by, he was down on the floor in an instant. Taharka could no longer see what was in his eyes.

But on the day of the rising of the Nile, most sacred day of all, when Taharka sat in solemn state high above the river in his sacred chair to bless the sacrifice—on this most sacred day Shabataka, in the throng of princes, raised his eyes to his, and nodded. Taharka, acknowledging the look as best as he could, felt his heart swell with relief.

Shabataka was still his brother.

⚒ 4 ⚒

The Journey

THE SUMMER of Taharka's sixteenth year was the same as any other. It was hot.

Taharka's studies in soldiering continued, though the priests did not approve—throwing the javelin, bending the Kushite longbow, cutting and slashing with the new iron-bladed swords. What wonders *they* were! Nothing could survive against them. They could bend bronze as if it were silver.

The weapons were full size now. Taharka's legs and arms and back were lengthening, his muscles beginning to ripple like a man's.

Other things were different, too.

Somehow he saw very little now of his uncle Embutah. When he though about it, he missed the old soldier's reassuring presence during practice time, missed hearing his rough voice calling out, "Too slow, Great God, too slow! Move your sacred back!"

Somehow, little by little, his brother Shabataka had taken over his training. It was fun to work with Shabataka who never seemed to get angry, who

31

patiently corrected his mistakes, then sat and talked with him as they sipped the unfermented grape juice and nibbled the unleavened honey cakes beside the lotus pool.

But, in any event, in this summer of his sixteenth year, Taharka's mind was on other things.

Preparations were being made for the journey, the great voyage down the Nile to Egypt, where he would become a married man.

It was on Shabataka's mind, too.

"And your name will finally be inscribed. On the stone. In the books of the priests."

He looked at his brother from the corners of his eyes—a strange, speculating look.

Taharka's mind was on something else.

"It's almost four years since I've seen Shepnu. What will I say to her?"

"Something formal," said Shabataka.

"It's strange, I don't really remember how she *looked* at all—just how I felt when they took her away."

"Well," said Shabataka, shrugging, "now you will have her back. For a little while. And meanwhile—" Again there was that veiled look.

"Yes," said Taharka. "I must choose my Companion."

Shabataka looked straight at him.

"Will it be me?"

Taharka felt a little shock. Long ago, it seemed, there had been no question. Of course it would be

Shabataka. But lately, for some reason, he had not
wanted to think about it.

"I don't know," he said.

Shabataka pretended to be hurt.

"Don't you trust me? Don't you think I can keep
the crops growing and the river flowing while you're
off having fun in the big city?"

"I don't know." He wasn't sure why he had said it.

The old, unreadable mask settled over Shabataka's
face. For just a moment, Taharka felt a little thrill of
warning.

But Shabataka only said, "I could do it."

The afternoon sun falling upon his dark shoulders
seemed to robe him in pride and dignity. Looking at
him, Taharka thought, as he had thought so many
times before: he should have been chosen. He had
been born to it.

So Shabataka became his Companion. He was
given the right to wear the white crown of Kush, to
carry the golden wand. The people would crawl to
him—as he had desired—and in his hands would
lie the fortunes of the land.

The day following the ceremony Taharka was carried in his sacred litter beneath his sacred umbrella
to where his sacred barge waited at the bank of the
sacred Nile. Because the barge was sacred his feet
were allowed to touch the deck, and he would be
able to move about freely. He drew a deep breath.
He would see all the sights.

It was a magical journey, 30 days from Napata to

Thebes and, to begin with, for the first time he saw
the great rapids. Four times in those thirty days the
current quickened and the barge was drawn up on
land to be dragged by teams of men past the wild
white waters churning over the rocks. Heave, heave,
heave, and the air was filled with a hymn of praise
to Pharaoh. Was it like this, he wondered, for Pi-
Ankhi the Great when he had sailed forth to make
Egypt one and glorious again?

At all other times the river was at peace and only
the banks teemed with life. There were great temples
all along the way, and there were the villages of the
farmers. The air hummed with water wheels crank-
ing up the Nile water, emptying it through sluices
into the ditches that kept the fields green. At night
it was full of the roar of the crocodile and the hippopotamus, sometimes of the lion and the hyena.
There were towns and trading posts and the bustling
cities of Karman and Dongola.

And, at the end of the final cataract, there was
the great island of the sacred hawk, for whom Taharka had been named, and he whispered to himself,
"Now we are in Egypt."

On the afternoon of the 30th day, they came to
Thebes. Taharka had grown up in a great city, but at
the sight of Thebes he blinked.

Two great walls rose before him, one on either
side of the river. They seemed to go on forever. Along
the raised banks of the river itself were two endless
lines of quays where the dock workers swarmed,

loading and unloading the river boats—grain, fruits, cloth, vegetables, all the produce of the river banks. Above the walls rose the flat roofs of houses, four or five stories high. And high above these glinted the gold-washed tops of needle-like red and white towers.

As they drew closer to the east bank, Taharka saw the faces. Many were near black like his own, others were the various shades of dark to medium brown he found among his cousins and brothers and sisters. But the stories were true. Here and there were faces the color of cream and hair of brown or red. Taharka shook his head. So this was Egypt.

They approached a great pier of white stone. He was placed upon his golden litter and the umbrella raised above his head. Trumpets of bronze sounded forth. Taharka had been shy of the people in this strange place; but they fell to their knees before him, faces to the ground, just as they would have done in Napata, and the same cries rose into the air: "Save us, Great God! Heal our ills, Son of the Sun! Nourish our grain, Bringer of the Nile! Destroy our enemies, Mighty Hawk!"

The powerful little men who carried the litter trotted through a gate in the towering brick wall. Trot, trot, trot, between brick warehouses and little brick wine shops. Through a great market place where fruits, vegetables, jewelry, charms and hexes, papyrus books, inks, and anything else, were sold under awnings of river reeds.

Then trot, trot, trot, into a great avenue paved
with brick and lined with crouching stone lions with
the heads of rams. Now he could hear the bleating
and lowing of the animals to be sold for sacrifice, for
the litter was approaching the temple of Amon, most
holy of all the houses of the god. The wall loomed
high. The litter passed through a towered gate and
Taharka thought he would be struck deaf by the
bawling and baa-ing, not to mention the cries of the
people.

Before him was a flight of steps, and on each side
a giant stone figure—giant images of that mighty
king Rameses II, that great god who had laid waste
the land of Canaan. Bump, bump, bump, up the steps,
and the terrible noise began to fade into something
like a far-off roar.

Now they were in the most immense room Taharka had ever seen, or even dreamt. The sun was
hidden by a roof so high above Taharka's head that
it was lost in shadows and he could not see it, much
less the tops of the mighty stone columns that sup-
ported it—columns to which Taharka and his attendants were like mice to men—columns painted and
carved with gods and kings and sacred animals, so
bright and beautiful even in the dimness that the
young king's eyes were dazzled.

There was the sound of singing in the great room.
Among the giant columns, down a kind of avenue
between them, came a procession of men with shaved
heads and white linen skirts. For a moment Taharka

lost some of his excitement and wonder. These men might have been priests in Napata; and, sure enough, they fell upon their knees and crawled to him, faces to the ground.

Led by the priests, Taharka's procession moved on, out of the hushed hall of the columns, into the sun again. And now Taharka's heart beat steadily faster, his eyes shone with awe. For ahead of him lay the dark walls of the oldest of all of Amon's houses, stretching back a thousand years or more, the true house of the god. And within those walls lay the red chamber, the most secret and hidden place of all —the holy of holies. Here lay the oldest of all the images of Amon; and the sacred box in which he was carried once a year, on his feast day. In all the world, only one person was allowed to see the inside of that chamber. That person was he—Taharka.

Of all the unbelievable things that was the hardest for Taharka to believe.

But first they turned off into a small chapel where the kings of the Two Lands made their offering to Amon. A spotless ram had its throat cut. All present drank a little of its sacred blood and had a little smeared on their foreheads.

It was then, looking away from the sacrifice, that he saw it. The figure on the litter, the layered headdress of linen and feathers. Not a human being, but a statue—except that he could see its eyes move, which frightened him because this was certainly a goddess. He remembered that the high priestess in

Thebes was more sacred than Pharaoh himself. Like Pharaoh, she wore the golden cobra coiled upon her brow. The crook and the flail were crossed upon her breast. The litter passed by him.

And then it came to him. That statue was Shepnuset.

What had they done to her? Was it Shepnuset at all? Terrible things were done in Thebes, he had heard. Had they locked her away somewhere, and substituted this frightening image of a stranger to terrify him into obedience?

A feeling of numbness settled over him. And then the high priest humbly asked him if he wished to greet his divine father. Humbly, but of course it was a command. He was being commanded to enter the holy of holies.

Suddenly Taharka turned cold with terror. *He* to enter the holy of holies? It was as if the past five years had never happened. He was not the god, he should never have been the god. It was all an accident. Amon knew it, if nobody else did. If little Taharka, the son of the Bantu slave girl, were to enter that red chamber, what would happen?

Amon would strike him dead, that was what would happen.

The high priest spoke again, more urgently, asking if it would please the Great God to come to his divine father. *Now.*

For the first time, here in this holy city, Taharka disobeyed the command of a priest.

Slowly, languidly, he tilted back his head, half closing his eyes.

"It does not please me. I will rest now."

And, after all, as Shabataka would have said, what could they do about it? The Great God had spoken.

In a silence shimmering with an undercurrent of shock they carried him from the offering chamber and from the ancient court, through other gates and passages, into the Great House of the king.

Taharka felt the numbness leave him. This was more like what he was used to. No giant chambers and pillars here. The rooms were no larger than his rooms in Napata, the cedar wood stools and tables, no finer. Even the great bed in the alcove had little more gold and silver on it than his great bed at home.

He stretched himself on that bed now. Silent servants drew red linen curtains across long, narrow windows and crept from the room. Never had Taharka felt himself so alone. Tears gathered beneath his eyelids. He realized that there was no one here that he knew. Shabataka and the priest of Sebek had chosen the attendants who would accompany him—some for their strength, some for their intelligence, some because they had traveled north before. Now Tarharka realized that he barely recognized any of them.

Anyway, he thought, what did it all matter? The day would come, it *must* come, when he would enter the holy of holies, lay his hands on the sacred image and place it in the sacred cask, to be carried in procession. And when that day came—who could save him then?

There was a little flurry at the door of the outer chamber, a whispering and, unbelievably, a kind of giggle. He sat up amazed, pushing aside the curtains of the sleeping alcove.

"Hari?"

It was not a little round girl who stood near the door. It was a tall, imposing young woman with innumerable black braids hanging over her shoulders, the tips tinted with gold. She wore a collar of gold around her neck.

But it was not a statue, not a goddess. It was Shepnu.

The first thing she said to him was: "Are you hungry?"

❦ 5 ❧

God and Goddess

TAHARKA rose to his feet and covered his emotion by falling into the Great House formalities that he had been so carefully taught. He inclined his head ceremoniously, as was due to the priestess of Amon. Then he replied in the manner proscribed.

"The God is indeed hungry!"

Shepnuset turned to the door and clapped her hands.

"It will be a minute," she said.

She drew closer, looking him over in wonder.

"The God has grown tall," she said at last.

"So has the Lady."

The hands that Shepnu extended to his were warm and eager.

They both were suddenly shy, but Shepnu couldn't be repressed for long. Her eyes glinted.

"Will the God not give the Lady the kiss of greeting?"

Taharka felt his face grow hot. "The Lady knows that that takes place before the people on the morrow.

41

Indeed, the God is surprised to see the Lady before then."

"Thebes is not Napata. The Lady goes where she likes."

He believed her. He felt sorry for those who had to keep her in check.

"So the Lady does not hate Egypt any more? What of the poppy smoke?"

Shepnu had tired of the game. "I've never breathed it! You think I'm a fool? I pretend, and they don't dare do anything about it, and—" she began to giggle. "The high priest of Amon: He asked me what Amon required, to remove the curse from his vineyards in the delta. I told him he must dress up in his wife's clothes and perform the priestess's harvest dance in front of the people." She smiled wickedly. "And he did it!"

Taharka's eyes widened. Then he realized that, instead of shuddering in horror, he wanted to laugh. He thought of the pompous high priest and actually did chuckle.

A platter of food was brought into the chamber. The servants crept out, heads down.

Taharka looked at the contents of the meal in disbelief.

"Fish? Fish roe? For *me*? You know it's forbidden."

"I have friends," she said. "They get things for me. And some of the priests turn their backs."

Taharka drew himself up. He had dared the gods

enough for one day. A ring of authority entered his voice. "The God is not pleased. Take it away!"

Shepnu shrugged and ordered something else.

As he ate, she drew up a stool and talked. There were stories of her pranks and misdeeds, but he noticed that as with him, the bright spots were only spots. Most of her life was unpleasant routine.

In a moment of silence he looked at her and said, "The God is indeed happy to see his Lady. You were missed in Napata."

Shepnu smiled, but then her lips grew hard.

"I will always be missed in Napata."

"What do you mean? We will always—

He stopped. Because, of course, they would not always be together.

The custom. The god in Napata. The priestess in Thebes. Sacred wife and god husband, but never together.

"It was his fault," said Shepnu. "Pi-Ankhi."

"Pi-Ankhi?" Taharka was puzzled. What did his half-brother Pi-Ankhi have to do with it?

"Pi-Ankhi the Great, *that* Pi-Ankhi. The first of our line. The Great! He was so great because he left his wife here in Thebes to rule as priestess, so he could go back to Napata and keep on being the god. *She* was so great they never changed the custom. It's their fault."

Taharka thought about this—about those strong women who, since the days of Pi-Ankhi, had ruled in Thebes like the old, all-powerful African queens in the stories. He thought about Shepnu and how she was now one of them. Little Shepnu. Could she do it? She had always been stubborn. Tough. And now—

She had changed. She was grown up.

So was he. Had he changed?

Not much, he thought. He still thought of himself as the captive "child god," the prisoner in the Great House. Not as a man or a king.

"You don't know how to be the god," Shabataka had said. Well, he had tried. He had failed today before the Holy of Holies. But if Shepnu could do these things, he could still try.

He put down his bowl and said, "The customs stand, O Lady, but two of us are stronger than one."

She nodded. Her movement caused her braids to swing. The little braids reminded Taharka of the ones he had pulled years before.

"Do you remember—" he began.

And suddenly they went back to being children again, recalling the old days in Napata, the games in the children's court, laughing at the old jokes.

"Remember Shabataka? Remember the time he put the snake in the sun priest's chalice?"

"I never liked Shabataka," said Shepnu.

In the middle of one of Shepnu's stories—something about a way she had found to get into the Holy of Holies and how, one of these days, she was going to do it—the god king fell asleep.

Shepnuset stood looking down at the tall, tired

boy. The laughter in her eyes had died away. They were grave and brooding, like the eyes of a mother. She half turned to the door to call for a servant, but changed her mind. She draped his arm over her shoulders and walked him, still sound asleep, to the alcove where he collapsed and rolled over onto the great bed.

Before she left, she bent down and kissed him.

❧ 6 ❧

Gathering Clouds

NO, TAHARKA decided, a month after his arrival, Thebes was not Napata.

The king had, for example, a food taster, to guard against poison. In Napata this would have been unthinkable. What assassin would dare target the god? Taharka couldn't believe the man was in any danger but didn't stir up trouble by getting rid of him.

He had kept his word to himself. He was learning how to be the god. He was staying awake at the council meetings, asking questions, watching the faces of the men who were his advisors. The Theban vizier seemed honest enough. As for the high priest of Amon, he could not read his face—until one day he reversed one of his judgments. The commanders of the army were easy to understand. They wanted action. They looked back in longing to the days of Egypt's glory. They look to the east and the north where a new shadow loomed, a shadow that had once been Egypt's.

The Assyrians!

More and more often the meetings seemed to center around news of the Assyrians. A new king in power. Another city threatened. The army commanders were angry—who were these upstarts to lay claim to the world that had once bowed before Egypt? Egypt was one again. How long before she awoke from her long sleep?

From the south came unsettling news, brought by messengers on swift horses riding right across the desert, the great Kushite bend of the Nile. It was sad news. Three good friends had died, all at once. The priest of Horus, a man most devoted to the young Taharka, who was named for his god, had choked on his food at dinner and could not be revived. The heart of Taharka's old tutor had failed, though it had never troubled him before the hour of his death. And then the vizier of Napata, a most just and honorable man, had ridden out to hunt the hippopotamus, and had not ridden back again.

Taharka was grieved. He had been fond of the vizier. He remembered the patient help of his old tutor, and the stories of the hawk god told by the kindly priest of Horus.

He would make special offerings at their tombs when he returned to Napata.

That evening he was offered a dish of the unspiced goose considered fit for Pharaoh. He refused it. Shepnuset had smuggled in more tempting (though still not forbidden) items and he had already dined.

The smuggled food saved his life.

The taster had already sampled some of the goose and had noticed nothing unusual, but that night he became very ill.

In the morning he was dead.

"It could have been spoiled."

Taharka could still not believe what had happened; though, for the first time in his life he was feeling the real, cold clutch of fear.

Gently, soothingly, Shepnuset stroked his hand. They were together on the rooftop garden, together as often as they could be, *while* they could be.

"No," she said, "He would surely have tasted *that!*"

Taharka rose suddenly. It was all becoming too much. Who was behind this horror? Who had dared? Had they been paid? At the meetings there had been talk of murders paid for by the agents of the Assyrians.

No, it was all too much.

"I can't do it!" he said suddenly. "It was all a mistake. How can I stand up to them all, make the decisions, now not even knowing who to trust. And without you—"

He stopped.

For that was the way things were. The marriage, the ritual, the union of the god with the divine priestess. Then—back to Napata. Alone.

"We're not supposed to love each other," said Shepnuset soberly.

"But we do!" he said, bitterly. And he knew it was true. It had always been true.

"Yes. We have that. That's something, isn't it?"

"No. People live with their wives. Everybody has someone to work with, make plans with, to be on his side. Everybody but us. Shepnuset . . . did you ever think of just running away?"

Almost to his surprise, Shepnuset said, "Yes."

"We could do it. Nobody knows our faces. I could work on the docks. My grandfather built boats!"

"You are not your grandfather," said Shepunset quietly. "You are the God King."

In Napata, the grizzled soldier Embutah knelt before the image of the serpent god. It was his favorite. It reminded him of the carved wooden image in the far-off, long-ago jungles of his childhood. For some reason, those far-away forests had been much in his mind that day. The village, its narrow lanes teeming with goats and fowl. His father, the boat builder. The joyous trips down the Zambezi to the market town on the eastern sea. The cargoes of oil and fish and palm wine. His little sister, with her big curious eyes and her love of stories. The happy days of yesteryear. The days now were not happy. The stories of the Assyrians. The whispering of the men who now surrounded the god's Companion, always silenced when he appeared. The arrogance of the Companion himself.

Should he warn his nephew? Of what should he caution him?

In the shadows, a dark figure hovered, a dagger gleaming in its hand.

※ 7 ※

Embutah!

PHARAOH sat upon his throne, the serpent scepter in his hand, the double crown upon his head, Shepnuset at his side.

He was very tired. His head spun with the events of the day—disputes to settle, requests for favors, ambassadors from Punt, from Sheba across the Red Sea.

The crier called one more name.

"Amos, son of Neriah, ambassador from Hezekiah, king of Judah."

Pharaoh's eyes widened. The man had approached the throne on his feet.

There was a soft, shocked hiss of breath from the people in the great hall.

Taharka leaned forward, no longer half asleep. The man was tall, brown, his black hair clubbed in a heavy braid. He was dressed like a traveler who has had no time to change. He moved like a prince, someone who would be at home in the courts of

51

kings, but was as lean and sinewy as a man of the desert. He bowed, for courtesy, when he approached the throne, then straightened and looked straight into the eyes of Pharaoh.

This time the people began to murmur, a few to cry out in horror. The vizier's voice rose above them.

"Where is your tribute, envoy? Your gifts for the God?"

The man made his reply to Taharka.

"I bring no gifts, my lord. I have come in great haste. What I have to say—"

Suddenly he swayed on his feet.

Thinking he was about to fall, Taharka rose.

"You are ill!"

The man steadied himself with his traveler's staff. But Taharka was remembering his lessons in healing at the school for the children of the god. The man's face was gray from exhaustion. Another few moments and he would collapse in earnest.

"Bring him into the small chamber," he ordered.

"And bring him some wine," said Shepnuset.

They made their way the length of the great hall to a small room set aside for private audiences. The vizier, more fearful than ever since the death of the taster, tried to follow, but Taharka waved him back. This man was in no condition to play tricks.

The door closed behind them and the man Amos, in his travel-stained robe, leaned against it. A deaf servant brought him a chair and helped him into it.

"Forgive me," said the man.

"Don't talk. Wait for the wine."

The wine was brought. After a while the grayish look left the man's face.

"A good night's sleep is all I need. I forget when I had one last. There hasn't been time."

Ambassador from Judah. Taharka was searching his mind, trying to remember. There had been a story, long ago. Embutah had told him a story.

"You have a sister kingdom, Israel?"

"Had," said Amos. "Israel is no more. We of Judah are all that is left of the Israelite tribes."

The voice of Embutah came back to Taharka: "Your father had no help to give. Israel hasn't been heard from since." Taharka settled into his own chair. He was curious to hear what the man had to say. Shepnuset put a question.

"Are you well enough to talk?"

He nodded.

"It's been many years since we have heard from Judah. Why are you here?"

"To bring you news. And a warning. And to ask for your help."

"The news first," said Shepnuset.

The man raised his eyes, dark and troubled, but with the glimmer of a fierce fire.

"Sidon has fallen to the Assyrians."

The Assyrians again. There was a stillness about Taharka's heart. Sidon, the great trading city across the desert of the east, on the northern sea. This was no idle news.

"Soon," said the man, "they will be in Judah."

"Why?" said Shepnuset. "Does not Judah send tribute to the Assyrians?"

For a moment the man's head drooped. Then, with some effort, he again raised his eyes.

"There comes a time," he said, "when people can bear no more."

From somewhere inside himself he seemed to be summoning new strength.

"When Israel fell, the father of my king hastened to send tribute to the Assyrians. He built an altar to the god of their city, Nineveh, and humbly begged the mercy of their king. For years we saw our children conscripted for their armies and their slave gangs, went hungry while our barley went to Nineveh, saw the silver drained from our treasury in Jerusalem. Then one day my king, my glorious King Hezekiah—"

Taharka, god king of the Nile, with the crown of the two kingdoms on his brow, could not help smiling just a little. Amos stiffened.

"My king, son of David in the thirteenth generation, said: 'Enough!' He looked around our beautiful city Jerusalem and said, 'I will make it clean again.' He sent word through Judah and the coast: 'No more! No more silver to build the stables and the temples of Nineveh. No more children taken away to serve the tyrant. No more tribute.' And then—" He smiled at the memory. "And then he smashed the altar to the Assyrian god."

The little room was very still. He's crazy, thought Taharka. So is his king. And yet, somehow, deep inside him he could feel a thrilling echo of the triumph in the voice of the man from Judah, the man whose king did not fear a foreign god.

"So," said the god king, "that is why they will soon be in Judah." He was sure they would, when they heard about that altar. And when the silver stopped coming in.

The man Amos tried to rise. He couldn't quite make it. But he leaned forward and his eyes, dark and intent, focused on the eyes of Pharaoh. Taharka could not look away.

"No, my lord, that is not the only reason. I said I had also come to bring you a warning. Listen well, my lord."

Aided by his staff, he did manage to struggle to his feet.

"The Assyrians have a new king. Sennacherib."

Taharka had heard the name.

"Make no mistake. Jerusalem means nothing to this man—a man still young, a greedy, ambitious man. His father conquered Babylon! What is Jerusalem to him? They have already robbed us of anything of value. No, to this new king, Jerusalem is only a snapping dog guarding a doorway—something that stands in his way."

A doorway, thought Taharka. A doorway to the gold in the mines of Kush.

A doorway to the green banks of the Nile.

The man Amos nodded as if Pharaoh had really spoken.

"Yes, my lord. My king—my city Jerusalem—we are all that stands between the nations of the Nile and a very dark night. And time is short. Even now Assyrian agents are being sent throughout the world, across the eastern desert. Already silver and gold has been paid out to men in high places. Rewards for treason and murder."

The lamps were flickering. The shadows really were gathering in the little chamber. Murder. The death of the taster. Men in high places. What men? Which high places?

The man from Judah collapsed suddenly into the chair.

"Forgive me," he said again. And again Taharka forgot everything else in his concern for the exhausted man.

"You must sleep," he said. "Even before food. We'll find you a bed in the outer courts. We'll talk about this—later."

"There isn't much time for talk!"

Taharka looked at him in wonder. This was a strange man indeed. He came here, desperate for help, but on his feet, looking the god in the face, speaking to him as if he were any ordinary man.

And now he seemed to be telling the god to hurry up and make up his mind!

"There is time," said Taharka soothingly.

He did not meet with Amos the next few days. He saw him once, rested and well again, a new fire in his eyes. No time, no time, his eyes seemed to be saying.

The news of Sidon's fall had become general knowledge. The council meetings grew loud. The general of the armies pressed and pressed: The time is right! They are occupied with other matters! An expeditionary force across the desert! If we miss this opportunity—

Only the high priest had nothing to say. His thoughts seemed to be focused on something else. There was something in his silence that chilled Taharka more than all the warlike talk. It seemed to stir that other thought that was pressing on his heart.

Somebody wants me dead.

A messenger arrived from Napata and demanded an audience with Pharaoh. He carried news that could not wait. He had made the journey in 14 days!

Taharka sat in his cedarwood chair in the private chamber of the god and heard what the messenger had to tell him.

There was a long silence. Then Taharka said: "Leave me."

And, when the man was slow to move: "Leave me! Now!"

The darkness in the chamber, lit only by a small lamp, was like a black robe smothering him. He began to cry. He fell upon the great bed in the alcove and beat the cushions and sobbed.

Embutah!

"This is a spear, my little nephew. You grasp it *so*—they were not gods, your mother's people, but they were fine people—too slow, Great God, too slow! Move your sacred back!"

Embutah, all he had left of his mother.

This time there was no question of the will of the gods. This had been no failure of the heart, no hunting accident.

The uncle of the god had been found with a knife in his back.

The little lamp flickered. Soon the oil would be burned away. Taharka watched it gutter.

So the Assyrians were there—even in Kush—striking down all that was honest and good to make way for that dark night of their own making.

Unless— For just a moment, a thought far down in his mind flickered upwards and gave him pause. But no, darkness like this could not arise from the green banks and life-giving water of his beloved Nile. He would not even think it.

A long time he sat without moving. Then he felt the anger. It welled up inside him like a bitter, gushing spring. The world was trembling. He was the god. He had been taught that it was up to him to keep it sane and steady. The Assyrians might be strong, but this was Egypt—Egypt that once had ruled the world! They would raise an army. One man out of every ten, armed with the iron-headed spears. Chariots and horses.

Just as he was, in the middle of the night, he sent for the men he needed—the vizier, the general. And Amos, the envoy from Judah.

"You can have your expeditionary force. You can have your war with the Assyrians. Send to Napata. I will meet with the council tomorrow."

And he thought to himself, I will go with them. I will see them pay for what they have done.

For the first time, the man from Judah knelt before the god king—not in worship, but in gratitude and relief. There were no misgivings in *his* eyes.

And the eyes of the general of the armies shone with an eager light.

❧ 8 ❧

The Smile on the High Priest's Face

THE GREAT GOD had spoken. Messengers on the fastest horses in the stables were sent south to Kush.

Shabataka would know what to do.

Chariots, from stables all along the Nile, began to roll in to Thebes. Word was sent to the iron smiths in every town and village to convert their shops into arms factories, to work through the night, hammering the spear heads and the arrow heads and the sword blades into shape. The order for conscription went out through the land of Egypt.

Taharka was tense as a tight drawn rope. When the army arrived from Kush, he was going to war. What did he know of foreign wars? For that matter, what did any of them know of this war they were going to fight? Who among them had ever faced the Assyrians—the Assyrians who had conquered Babylon? Who among them knew anything about them, outside of children's stories and wild rumors passed along from mouth to mouth? The general of the armies was as ignorant as he himself.

Taharka sent for Amos. Amos might tell them what they would have to face.

"I've never faced them. But I know a man who has."

"Here? In Thebes? Bring him to me."

The man Amos brought to him was the most outlandish person Taharka had ever seen. He was a man still young. His face was fair, what he could see of it. It was partly covered by a beard of golden brown, which was also the color of his hair. His eyes were blue. Taharka had never before seen a blue eyed man.

"This is Talos," said Amos. "He comes from a town called Corinth. Across the Sea of the North."

It was obvious that Talos, unlike the man from Judah, thought that Taharka just might be a god. He was taking no chances. He was down on his knees, staring hard at the floor.

"How do *you* come to know so much about the Assyrians?" the king asked him.

Careful not to look too far upwards, the man ventured to reply.

"I am a trader, Great One. Pottery, bronzes, dyes —some ironware, too," he added proudly. "I go everywhere. I speak all the tongues. I was in the city of Samaria, capital of Israel, when the Assyrians struck. I was younger then or I might not have come out alive."

Taharka leaned forward.

"Tell me," he said.

Talos spread out his hands. He closed his eyes, as if conjuring up a picture buried in his mind.

"Row upon row, column upon column of men. They covered the horizon, they blotted out the sun. Spearmen, bowmen, swordsmen—all iron swords!—pikemen, slingers. They wore shirts of iron scales. And the horses! Not just chariots, but men on horseback who can strike where they will."

Horse soldiers. We could do that, thought Taharka. Our messengers ride horses. We could get new horses, find men to train them—if we had the time!

"And towers. Towers on wheels."

"Towers? On wheels?"

"They carry great, pointed battering rams. No wall, no gate can stand against them. And on top of the towers stand archers who can pick off the defenders on the wall like ducks."

"They will be of no use against us," said Taharka, though for a moment he felt chilled. "We will meet them in the open."

"Spoken like a king," said Amos. "But you must know the odds. The numbers."

"How many men can the Assyrian king bring up against us?"

"I have heard that he commands a hundred thousand."

Taharka could bring up twenty thousand from Kush. Here in Egypt, it was not sure.

"We must double the conscription," he said. "Two men out of every ten."

"And there will be our Philistine vassals," said Amos. "The men of Askelon, Ekron, Gath."

Talos shook his head sadly.

"I have not yet told you what happened to Samaria. The walls—thick as the height of a tall man—were smashed like egg shells. The Great House of Hosea the king was gutted by fire, the houses burned to the ground. I saw the great men of the city herded into the square and slain, impaled on stakes. I saw all the people of the town, the children too, with ropes around their necks, herded out at the heels of the army. I myself only escaped because I amused them, an alien barbarian with pale eyes. May I never come so close again!"

There was silence in the chamber of the god.

For a moment Taharka was back in Napata, listening to Embutah. "They cut down young trees and put our necks in the forks with a bar of iron across, and roped us together—"

But those men had not been the men of Assyria. Those men had been the men of Kush.

He shivered. Evil was evil, wherever it arose. And this evil was the evil of the Assyrians.

He beckoned Talos close.

"Now," he said, "I will call in my army advisors. You must think back. You must think hard. I must have more than this. You must tell me everything you can remember, how they were commanded, how they were deployed. I must have numbers, I must know how they will attack—"

The men met far into the night while the trader from Corinth searched his memory, back over the years.

Later, the darkness of Talos' story hung over Taharka like a heavy shadow. Perhaps that was why the real shadows of the Great House seemed sinister that next day, why the smile on the face of the high priest of Amon somehow chilled him, why there even seemed a touch of insolence in the manner of the captain who guarded his chamber.

He shook off the feeling as well as he could.

Even now, there were other things to think about.

For—all of a sudden, it seemed—the time of the great ceremony was upon them. In three days, he would be a married man.

He was sixteen years old and he knew that, deep down, he was a little frightened. But his love for his childhood companion helped him now. The future was dark and confused. Danger and strife and terrible loneliness lay ahead. But for a little while, at least, he would be happy. He would wrap himself in a magic spell of happiness.

He and Shepnu saw each other that afternoon for the first time in several days. They were to make the final offering before the ceremony, to the image of Isis, goddess of marriage.

And there, before the image, the spell was broken.

"Hari," said Shepnu, and only he could hear her, "I'm afraid."

The fear in her voice was not like his fear, the fear before the marriage.

This was a cold fear, like the smile on the high priest's face.

He waited. As the voices rose in the chant, she whispered again.

"I've heard something. I have to talk to you, but I think they're watching me."

The thought of the dead taster drifted though Taharka's mind.

"Try to come tonight," he said. "And—" He stopped. For this was the worst of all. Among all of them out there—advisors, servants, guards—there was no one he was sure he could trust.

"Bring Amos with you."

Something seemed to have spoken for him.

❧ 9 ❧

Nightmare

H E WAITED that night, for Shepnuset, waiting with foreboding. The words of Amos rang in his head. Treason and murder. Men in high places.

There was a soft breeze from the river, making the lamps flicker and the shadows dance. He looked about the chamber. He touched the little tables, touched his special chair. He took comfort in the strong, smooth wood.

He had a strange feeling, as if he were saying goodbye. A hawk had cried that night, after the dark. Was it an omen?

What was the matter with him? Nothing had happened. This was a night like any other. It would be many days before the army arrived from Kush. There were many days of happiness in this chamber left to him.

Where was Shepnu?

There were voices outside, the voice of the guard captain.

"No one is permitted to speak to the God tonight."

He could not believe what he had heard. He was across the room in an instant and at the door, flinging it wide.

Amos was there and, in the shadows, Shepnuset. Facing them, barring their way, was the captain.

He had drawn his sword.

"How dare you?"

At the sound of Taharka's voice, the captain swung around. He fell back a little, instinctively shielding his eyes.

"How dare you draw your sword before the priestess of the sun?"

The man was cringing now, but Taharka could sense again that shadow of insolence, stronger now.

"I have had my orders."

"Give me the sword."

The man hesitated.

"On your knees!"

Slowly the man collapsed. (What will become of the god when men no longer fear him? Embutah had said.) He held out the sword. Taharka took it from his hand, staring at it as if at some strange and alien object.

Amos spoke for the first time. "Bring him inside."

Taharka gestured with the sword. The man sidled into the room. The others followed.

"My lord," said Amos. He was holding out his

hand, never taking his eyes from the captain. Taharka, with a sudden shudder, handed him the sword.

"Go to the window, my lord. Look down into the court."

Taharka crossed the chamber and drew back the long red draperies, looking down to where his guard patrolled. A feeling of nightmare settled over him.

"Those are not my guard," he said. "I've never seen them before."

"And there are a great many of them," said Amos grimly. He touched the captain with the sword.

"Who gave you your orders?"

"My high captain of a hundred."

"And who gave them to him?"

The man was thoroughly cowed now. "I don't know. I don't know anything else. I swear."

"He's lying," said Amos.

"It doesn't matter," said Shepnuset. "I know where the orders came from."

"Tell us what you know, my lady. We may not have much time."

"I was in Isis's chapel. I heard two priestesses whispering. One of them was the wife of the high priest. I heard her say: 'It will not be a sacrilege. Not before the marriage. Besides, this one was never the god.' And the other one said: 'Even gods fall sometimes. We are *your* servants, lady, and the servants of our lord the high priest.' I didn't understand, but it frightened me. What does it mean?"

"It means," said Amos, "that the king is in grave danger." His voice was low and tense, as if he were repeating the climax of an old, familiar story. "It means that there is treason in the highest places in the land. It means that whatever is to happen must happen before the marriage, and the marriage is in two days, and this very night Pharaoh's guard has been replaced by strangers. It means that my lord must leave this place. Tonight."

Taharka stared at him.

The hawk. An omen. A true omen?

He felt numb. He felt nothing at all. This was not really happening.

Shepnuset said, "I will call my bodyguard. They will defend him."

"Too few and too risky," decided Amos. "He must flee the danger."

The captain was edging toward the door. Amos swung upon him, sword in hand.

"Don't move," he said. And to Taharka, "We will need some rope."

"The curtains," said Taharka. With a small knife from one of the tables, he sliced off a length of cord.

"Can you tie a safe knot?" said Amos. The sword was at the captain's throat.

"I can do it," said the king.

He bound the captain's arms behind him. He had made a good job of it, he thought, as if he were watching someone else. It was as if someone outside him were telling him what to do—Embutah, or his warrior fathers. For a moment it did not even seem strange.

Amos looked about the chamber. There was a chest of ebony, its lid weighted with the image of a hippopotamus. Amos, with Shepnu's help, removed the lid.

"Inside," he said to the captain. And the captain, as best he could with his bound arms, clambered in. The lid was set back in place.

"They'll find him," said Amos. "But not too soon."

The three of them stood still, looking at each other.

"All the doors will be guarded," said Taharka at last. "How do we get out?"

"If I had known," said Shepnu, "I would have brought Kefmose."

"Kefmose?"

"The guard at the holy of holies. I saved him once when the high priest would have had him beaten and he fought them. Now he does whatever I command. He says he was once a cat burglar."

Taharka had a crazy urge to laugh. A cat burglar!

But Amos's eyes had brightened.

"A cat burglar. Yes! And there is a story of our great king, David. They sent assassins one night to watch him and slay him in the morning. But his wife came to warn him. She let him down through a window, and so he escaped."

"The windows lead down into the court."

"We must go over the roof."

Amos was at the windows already. Rip, rip, rip. The long red draperies, high as the shadowed ceilings, came tumbling down.

"The cords, too. Bed linens. Get to work, great lady. To work, my lord. We have no time."

They set themselves to the task at hand, gathering what they could find. They tore and twisted and knotted until a rope began to emerge.

"Pull, pull!" said Amos. "The knots must hold."

"Will it be long enough?" said Shepnu.

"It will have to be."

There was a stirring in the courtyard.

"Look down, my lord. See what is happening."

Taharka stood in the shadows by the window.

"A priest is there. He's talking to them. Now they are talking among themselves. Now they are still. Their captain has given them an order." He stiffened suddenly. "They're moving inside!"

"So," said Amos. "Time has run out. Whatever is to happen will happen soon. Roll up our ladder. It's time to go. Get rid of your jewels, my lord."

"My jewels? My rings? My sacred collar?"

"Everything. Your face is not known—I thank my God now for that tabu! There must be nothing to identify you."

Taharka stripped them off.

He stood in the middle of the chamber of the god.

A god no longer, just an ordinary Kushite boy in his simple linen kilt. He could not believe this was real.

But Shepnu was real.

For just a moment the old dream of freedom stirred him, like a breeze from the river.

"Shepnu," he said. "Come with me. This is our chance! The only chance we'll ever have to be together. This is our chance to try!"

But practical, irreverent Shepnu, who laughed at the tabus, at the formal speeches and intricate ceremony, shook her head.

"The people. I'm the priestess," she said simply.

"Then I will stay too. I am Pharaoh."

"Hari, they will kill you, and then what good will you be? But, whoever they are, they wouldn't dare touch me. I was born what I am. You're not consecrated yet. . . ."

"My lord," said Amos, "you must come. Quickly."

"Besides," said Shepnu. "Somebody has to be here to fight them. Somebody has to search them out. And," she said fiercely, "you *will* be consecrated, you *will* return. When the army arrives from Kush!"

Yes, the army. Shabataka his brother. He had forgotten. It would not be too long before his men would arrive.

"My lord," said Amos. "One way or another, we have to go. Now."

"Yes, now." Shepnu was urging him toward the stairs. "Go, and," she gestured toward the ebony box, "when you have had enough time, I will tell them where to find this one. A *long* time," she added grimly.

"Come, my lord," said Amos, "Save yourself so that someday you may see her again. Hurry, or we're both lost."

The makeshift rope coiled over his shoulder, he led the way to the stone staircase. Like someone in a dream, Taharka followed him. He felt lost, outside himself. Someone else was walking in his body. He saw Shepnu, the tears on her face.

Then she passed out of sight.

They must not be seen from the ground. Crouching low, they crept to the wall at the edge of the roof. Beyond it was another roof leading to the outer wall of the Great House, down into the great temple complex.

"We'll have to jump. Can you make it?"

He remembered Embutah. "A soldier has to jump streams and gorges. Practice the long jump. Every day a little farther."

He could make it.

He *just* made it. Amos caught him as he teetered on the edge. Yes, this is real, he thought, shaking, as he stared down into the space between the roofs.

"No time," said Amos, "no time." He led the way to the edge of the second roof.

Far below were the gardens of the sacred precinct. People—priests, altar boys, worshippers—wandered about, to and fro, absorbed in their own affairs.

"What if they see us?" whispered Taharka.

"Why should they look up?" said Amos. "Besides, with the torches down there, they can't see much up here. The light blinds them."

There was a niche in the wall near the corner. If you pressed close enough to the wall, it too offered some protection from the eyes below. Here, around a small image of Horus built up from the wall, Amos attached the rope. Taharka was in no mood to object to the sacrilege. Besides, Horus the Hawk had always been his special deity. Perhaps he would protect him now.

"Wait till I reach the ground, then follow," said Amos.

Slowly, hand over hand, muscles straining, Amos went down the "rope." On and on. Forever, it seemed to Taharka. Was it long enough? Would it hold?

It held and it was long enough, though he could see that Amos had to drop some distance before he hit the ground. He was not hurt. He looked up, nodded and beckoned him down.

Taharka grasped the rope. He could feel it wavering, his feet clutching desperately for the wall. They found it, then instinctively grasped the rope. He felt steadier. The shaking quieted. He could do it. His hands and feet were telling him what to do.

Down and down, never looking at the ground. The thoughts raced in his head. Had they come to the chamber? Had Shepnu told them he was sleeping and must not be disturbed? Would they dare to

face her down? Shepnu! Would she be safe? Would
he ever see her again? The Assyrians! He must come
through this. He must stand against them.

He had come to the end of the rope. Now he
must look down, gauging the distance. It seemed a
long way down. But, again, he had no choice. He
whispered one prayer to Horus and let himself drop.

His whole body was jarred and shaken, but he
knew at once that he was unhurt. Nothing was broken, nothing injured. Amos helped him to his feet.

They stood for a moment in the shelter of the
niche while Taharka got his breath and the strength
returned to his shaking legs.

"How are you, my lord?"

"I don't know. Strange. I've never felt like this
before. What are we going to do?"

"First of all," said Amos, "when we leave this wall
you are no longer my lord. You are no longer Taharka." And he added, "What name will you have?"

This isn't real, thought the young god. No, this
won't last long. The army will be here soon. They'll
search out this little nest of traitors, paid by foreign
spies. There will be a terrible uproar when they find
that I am gone. And when they hear that I'm
alive—

Still—for now. He thought of Shepnu and Shabataka, of the name they had always called him. He
thought of his special deity. After all, in a way this
was an adventure. For however long, he would make

the most of it, think of it as a kind of game, sent by gods to test him.

"Call me Haru," he said at last.

"Haru. Hawk," said Amos. "A good name, my— Haru. So here we go. Out into the world."

❧10❧

The House of Talos

NOBODY noticed them at all. People milled about, eyes on each other or on the ground. They never looked their way. Taharka was jostled—*jostled!*—by a young priest who then asked why he didn't look where he was going.

After recovering from the shock of this, he began to wonder what was going to happen.

"What now?" he asked. "Where do we go from here?"

"I haven't had time to think," admitted Amos. "We can't go to my lodgings. *I* can't go to my lodgings. I'm the first one they'll look for. Talos." Then he shook his head. "No. I brought him to you once. They will remember. They are very thorough."

They looked at each other. For the first time Amos seemed as much at a loss as the boy.

Taharka looked around him.

"Does it seem strange to you," he said, "how peaceful everything is?"

It was true. A peaceful, drowsy night on the Nile. The stars above as bright as ever.

Not that it was quiet. There was a constant hum of voices, even at this hour, broken sometimes by shouts and laughter. They had left the Sacred Precinct now and were in a world totally strange to Taharka—a world he had seen only rarely and always from high above on a litter or, when he was a child, from a chariot—a world of narrow streets and alleys, blank brick walls hiding who knew what within, little shops and stalls outside.

Taharka's stomach had begun to gnaw. They stopped at a stall and bought onions and cucumbers between thick slabs of bread.

"Never mind what's in it," said Amos. "You eat to live now, young Hawk."

Taharka tightened his lips, looking down at the tabu food. But, he reminded himself, he was the god. For now, the god would make his own rules. It wasn't forever anyway. He resolutely bit into the bread. Nothing happened, the earth stayed still.

Amos paid with some of the small-change beans in his money bag. Taharka felt a sudden shock. Money. Never before this night had the thought of money even occurred to him. For the first time he began to understand his plight. No, this was not a game. What was he going to do?

Where, for example, would he sleep that night? The shocks of the evening had begun to tell on him. His whole body craved sleep.

"We could find an inn," said Amos. "But better to save what we have. Who knows what I will find when I return to my lodgings—if I dare return at all! The homeless sometimes sleep down by the docks and the soldiers turn their backs. It's safe enough. We'll go there."

The homeless. Taharka, Son of the Sun, God King of Egypt and Kush, had become one of the homeless.

He followed Amos to the docks, his feet dragging, hardly noticing where they went. And there, on the stones, the lapping of the Nile in his ears, he slept.

He woke to the sun and the blue eyes of Talos staring into his.

He blinked, shook off the cover of sleep, and said the first thing that came into his head.

"What are you doing here?"

And then he thought: what was he, Taharka, doing here? Then he knew, and wanted only to sleep again.

Amos had awakened at once, sprung to his feet and reached for the knife at his belt. He let it go when he saw who it was.

"Yes," said Talos. "I thought this might be it."

He was munching on a piece of bread. He gave some to Amos and some to Taharka.

"Soldiers came to my house before the sun was up. They told me nothing, just tramped around, smashing everything in sight. When they found nothing, they left."

He swallowed the bread and wiped his fingers on his robe.

"So," he said to Amos, "after they had gone I went to your house to see if you knew what was happening. A good thing I went quietly! There they were, the same thing again. I hid and waited while they went through your place, and I saw there was no sign of you. They didn't say much. I thought they looked frightened. And, when everything was quiet, I began to think."

He leaned toward them, tapping his forehead.

"Now what, I thought, do Amos and I have in common that would interest the temple guards? And it came to me that there was only one thing. It was you, Great One."

"You musn't call me that now," said Taharka. "My name is Haru."

Talos nodded wisely.

"I understand," he said. "We have had our uprisings, our murders of chiefs and kings. I thought of that, then I thought: What if they were not looking for a thing, but a person? And if that person were a person never seen by humble human eyes, where might it be safe for that person to go? To a crowded place, of course, a humble place. And so I came down here."

He nodded triumphantly, looking very pleased with himself.

"It would have been safer for you, not to have come," said Amos somberly.

Talos shook his head.

"They're not interested in me. They were just taking no chances. With you, Amos, it is different. I would not go to your lodgings if I were you. They will be back."

He stood up, shaking the crumbs out of his robe. "You had better come with me."

Before Amos could speak, Taharka shook his head.

"Amos must do as he likes. But I will not have you in danger because of me."

"He will be in more danger from *me*, Haru," said Amos. "Think. Outside the Great House, how many have seen your face? Even when they carried you through the streets, they never saw you. Their eyes were on the ground."

"Where I am staying," said Talos, "they are not concerned with what goes on in the Great House. Their minds are on other things. They will think nothing of either of you."

"Has there been any news from the Great House? Any great outcry? The god is gone, we are all lost?"

"Nothing at all," said Talos. "I went to the Precinct before I came here. Everything goes on as usual."

Taharka felt chilled. Hardly anyone, he realized, even knew he was gone. The power of the high priest of Amon was very great. And Shepnu—had they shut her away, where she could not speak?

And he was not there to help her. "They will kill you," she had said, "and then what good will you be?"

None whatsoever.

"Come with me," said Talos. "After all, you have no other choice."

The house of the Corinthian trader was in a sort of suburb beyond the city where skilled workmen lived and foreigners sometimes stayed. It seemed incredibly small to Taharka. But it was a comfortable enough little house of white-washed brick with a red wooden door and a floor of earth. In the entry court a goat and a donkey were tied and a woman, a servant provided with the house, was grinding the wheat for the bread. There were three rooms, a little store room and a kitchen with a hearth and an oven.

After all, thought Taharka, looking around him, what more did a man really need?

Right now it was in a state of chaos, littered with fragments of vases, figurines and pottery smashed by the soldiers in their grim search.

Talos ignored this for the moment and showed them to one of the two smaller rooms.

"This is yours," he said. "Do what you like with it." He called to the servant woman to bring them some of the goat's milk.

Taharka was somehow shamed by the man's kindness.

"You are good to take us in," he said. "It won't be for long." And to Amos, "We'll find a messenger. Talos must know someone he can trust. I'll send to the Great House, let my friends know I'm safe, tell them to send to Napata—"

"No!" said Amos. And, at Taharka's startled look—
"*They* may have spies even in Kush. We must wait for
the army." And he added softly, "I think it will not be
long."

"How long?" said Taharka. "I cannot live as a beggar."

"As to that," said Talos, "as you say, nothing is
forever. When my lord is back in the Great House—"
he winked. "Then he can reward me."

"Nevertheless," said Amos, "we will pay our way."

Talos was curious.

"How?"

"For a start, this," said Amos.

He laid his money bag—the rings and the beans
—on the table. He noticed Talos was looking around
at the litter the soldiers had left, shaking his head in
despair.

"We'll help," said Amos. And the three of them
set to work to clean up the room.

Taharka had truly become Haru.

❦ 11 ❦

Physician

THE FIRST word from the Great House was
that the marriage had been postponed. Pharaoh was ill and under the care of his physician. But
the people were not to be disturbed. The ceremony
would be held soon.

They can't keep this up forever, thought Taharka.
They've gotten themselves into a trap. When the
army arrives from Kush—

But when that would be was uncertain; Amos's
money bag was getting flat. Amos himself was strangely silent. He seemed wrapped in his own thoughts.

"What will you do?" said Taharka. "Will you go
home? You came here on a mission. You've done
what you could."

And, whatever else, Amos's mission seemed to
have been a success. Preparations for the war against
the Assyrians seemed to be proceeding. Men were
being called up from the villages and the great es-
tates—two out of every ten as Taharka himself had

commanded. The Temple troops, the Treasury troops, the mercenaries, were marched out into the desert for the rigorous training under the blazing sun. The streets were seldom without the sound of a drum and the sight of a squad of men.

But Amos said only, "My mission has been—interrupted. I will stay a while."

It's because of me, thought Taharka. He's waiting to see what will happen to me. Why does he care?

What *will* happen to me? And he answered himself: When the army arrives from Kush, it will be over. They will find the traitors, and I will be back in the Great House. Safe. No worry about gold rings and bags of beans.

And then the unthinkable: What if it never happened? What if this were all that was left to me? What would I do?

Strangely enough it was Talos, returning from the markets, who provided an answer. He settled his packs, talking softly to himself, a habit of men who traveled and lived alone.

"Poor Baku."

"Who's Baku?"

"A man I met down on the docks. He's a physician there, to the longshoremen. Not much money, but it's a living. Only now his apprentice has been conscripted. He doesn't know where he's going to find anyone else, down on his luck, with a scribe-school education."

Very slowly, Taharka sat up. His eyes were very wide. "Down on his luck with a scribe-school education."

"Where is this man?" he asked.

"You have read the papyrus on the heart and the blood? You have read the papyrus on surgery?"

"I have studied them. At scribe-school in Kush." Taharka added honestly, "I'm not sure how much I remember."

The little brown man with the shaved head and the linen kilt studied him closely.

"That doesn't concern me," he said. "You would only assist me, always under my direction at first. You would study at night, of course. You would memorize all the incantations, all the prescriptions."

There was a long silence. Taharka glanced around the white-washed room with its basins and instruments. His heart was beating very fast. Outside he could hear all the hurry and bustle of the docks, the wash of the river against the boats, the flapping of sails, the shouts of the foremen.

"Very well," said the man at last. "We will try you."

Next day, a man came in with the tooth ache. Baku tested his apprentice.

"What poultice will bring down the swelling?"

And Taharka, searching his mind from his studies of the night before, rattled off the formula.

"Mix it," said Baku.

A woman, the wife of one of the foremen, came in, very upset. She had only had three children, she said, and already her hair was turning gray.

Taharka looked through the papyrus on cosmetics, mixed a rinse, and sold it to her, with instructions on how to apply it at home.

Then he was left alone in the surgery. A man had been injured on one of the boats from Memphis and could not be moved, and Baku had been called to the scene. As Taharka was using the time to brush up on a certain magic formula that had baffled him, another man was carried into the room, bloody and moaning with pain and fear. An emergency! What was he to do?

But it might have been the boatman on that long-ago crocodile hunt, the same wound, but gotten in a knife fight, not from the teeth of Sebek. And here everything was at hand—the splints, clean cloths, needles and threads to sew the wound.

The man went out on his feet, bowing and smiling, uttering his thanks and his relief.

"Thank you, doctor! Thank you, doctor!"

Doctor! Taharka, who had been called a god, stood smiling foolishly, in amazed self-satisfaction.

He ambled home that night in a haze of good feeling, humming a tune to himself. It was a love song. But that reminded him of Shepnuset. So he switched to one of the sailors' chants that he heard every day on the docks.

At a corner, he collided with a man who seemed to be waiting for someone. It was Taharka's fault. His mind had been on other things.

"Sorry! Are you all right?"

The man bowed low but not before Taharka had seen his face. The scar on it made it one that would easily be remembered. The man did not speak.

After a moment, Taharka looked back. The man was gone. Whoever he was waiting for, he seemed to have found him.

﹦12﹦

Shabataka, My Brother

NO WORD came from the Great House. The people *were* disturbed. Pharaoh had not come out in the morning to bless the Nile. Where was the daily report?

"They're hiding something. Is Pharaoh, the gods forbid, dead?"

"It will happen soon," Amos muttered to himself. "It will have to happen soon."

That evening he returned to the house of Talos without his gold rings and bracelets, loaded down with sacks of barley and non-perishable foods, enough for a journey.

"You're leaving?" said Taharka. Already he felt a strange, painful sense of loss.

"No," said Amos. "Not quite yet."

He would say no more.

And then the army arrived from Kush.

Taharka, in Baku's surgery, first heard them in the distance. The drums, the rattling of the spears on the great Kushite shields. Already the earth seemed to shake to their sound. For a moment his heart stopped, then pulsed again to that majestic beat.

They're here. They're here.

And, "They're here!" shouted a man, bursting into the surgery. "They're massing outside the city. There's a whole contingent of them—it looks like thousands —coming toward the docks.

How had they come so soon? It was only seven days since he had sent the message, and a horseman would take at least fifteen days to reach Kush. Had they been waiting somewhere not too far from the city? For what? Why?

Louder and louder. Yes, they were coming. A little boy, having a scraped knee treated—he had a nervous mother—suddenly slid off the table and ran to the door. Baku and Taharka looked at each other and, without words, followed his example.

They were coming. Line upon line of the tall, black men of Kush in their linen kilts, with their man-high shields, covered with the skins of beasts. They marched along the docks, filing out to block off the quays. All but one, the great main pier where the official barges were moored. The people followed slowly, curious, unsure of what was happening, a little frightened. A few tried to follow onto the pier, but were held back by the spears.

Taharka looked up. The tops of the houses nearby were swarming with people hoping for a better view. But this did not last long, for a soldier on horseback rode back and forth, shouting: "Into your houses! Clear the roofs on pain of death!"

"What is this?" whispered Baku. "What are they doing? Their general is coming? By boat?"

They had left an opening at the end of the quay. Through the gap Taharka saw a giant boat approaching. For a moment he thought it was the royal barge, but that could not be. No, it was indeed the barge of the general of the Kushite armies but, for some reason, was fitted out with the royal standards, leafed in gold. A soft murmur, like a sigh, rose among the people as the barge was moored and a small guard of men assembled. A great chair, washed in gold and resting on cedar poles, was lifted to the shoulders of four of the tall, tall men of the far south. In it sat not a general, but a god. He wore the double crown of the north and the south. He carried the golden wand.

"On your knees!"

The people obeyed, Taharka among them.

A man, the crier, had come out upon the landing. He carried a papyrus scroll which he slowly unrolled.

"I will read to you the words of the God. Let them be proclaimed throughout the city.

" 'I Shabataka, Son of the Sun, Great God of Kush, Lord of the Two Lands, do hereby proclaim my kingdom. This day a great sacrilege has been averted. Blasphemers have dared to claim my holy office in the name of a pretender, and because of this, the Assyrians have risen in the east and all manner of

evil has come upon the land. Let this sacrilege be
blotted out from memory. Let my divine rule be written from the day of my divine father's going forth. I,
Shabataka will cleanse the land of this blasphemy. I,
Shabataka will lead you against the Assyrians till
there is not one left to rise against my majesty.' "

"Let it be proclaimed." The man rolled up the
papyrus and stepped back onto the barge.

Silence hung over the quay, as still as the air itself.
No cries, no cheers, no exclamations of wonder rose
from the crowd. All that could be heard was the soft
lap, lap of the river against the stones.

Shabataka, thought Taharka. Not the Assyrians.
Shabataka. My brother.

The chair carriers, with their awesome burden,
were moving onto the landing. They were coming
closer. Taharka had only one thought:

He would not abase himself here on the stones
while his mortal enemy passed by.

Slowly he rose to his feet, his eyes on the radiant
figure in the golden chair.

There was a stirring among the soldiers, but they
would not move as Pharaoh passed them. As it moved
beyond him, the godlike figure turned its head.

He saw Shabataka's eyes widen in recognition.

He realized what he had done. He was in grave
danger.

As the god passed, the people had risen behind
him. Taharka moved back into the throng. He wanted
to run, but knew that this would be a fatal thing. He

listened, his heart racing for Shabataka's shout of command, but heard nothing. His thoughts churned. Shabataka had been surprised, he told himself, that was why there was no word of command.

Back, farther into the crowd till he was quite lost among them. The soldiers were moving now, spear points leveled, scanning the throng for the one who had dared stand on his feet before the god. But it was half-hearted. In all that shifting of men, women and children, who could say which one it had been?

Tonight it will be different, he thought. He knows now. He knows I am alive, he knows I am in the city, he knows I dared to face him. He will send men to search the houses in the district. I can't go back to Baku.

And, with all the rest, one thought throbbed in his brain, a great grief rising to overwhelm him:

Shabataka. Shabataka. I have lost my brother. I'm alone.

☙ 13 ☙

Flight From Thebes

IN THE HOUSE with the red door, Talos listened, amazed. Not an Assyrian plot after all? He would have believed anything of those monsters. And his own brother? Well, who would have thought it?

But Amos was not surprised. He had thought all along it might be true. This was what he had waited for.

"Brothers have risen up against brothers before. We have had our Cains and Abels."

"But Shabataka. He was my friend, my teacher. After Embutah, he was like my father."

"Yes," said Amos. "He has a sickness, a greed for power above everything else. He is very dangerous, and not only for you, my lord. This is what I have feared. Even if some miracle delivers Judah from the Assyrians, with such a man as Shabataka on the throne of Egypt, will the men of Judah ever live in peace?" He got to his feet. "They will come here

94

now for certain. I've known it was coming. There is no place they will not search, and search again. We must leave the city. All of us."

Taharka felt a deep shame.

"Forgive me, Talos," he said.

"It was my choice to bring you here. Besides, I have done as much business in Thebes as I can. It's time I moved on."

"Tonight," said Amos. "We must leave tonight."

It was true. If the soldiers came, they would probably come before dawn. Even now they might be fanning out over the city—quietly, of course. They would not want to cause too much stir.

They worked in feverish haste, gathering together what possessions they would be able to take. Taharka had little enough! Talos gathered as many of his trade goods as he was able into two sacks. Most must be left behind. He had only the one donkey tethered in the court. He had traded the others, hoping to get a better deal when his business was completed. It was too late now. The goat would come too, and as much grain and as many vegetables as they could carry. Taharka thanked the gods for Amos' foresight. They would not starve.

Hermes, the donkey, was loaded down with the sacks. They stood for a moment in the entry way, while Talos said a silent farewell to his possessions.

"A pleasant place," he said sadly. "A pleasant city. A great city! The greatest city I will ever see."

Amos was scanning the streets outside. His gold rings and bracelets gone, he wore his plainest garments—a simple Phoenician or Syrian tradesman. But Taharka thought that he still looked like a proud foreign prince—someone who should travel with his retinue, chartering a swift boat to carry him to his destination. Not someone who should creep out of the city at night with a wandering tradesman and—himself. What was he now? A donkey boy?

"I'm sorry," he said again. "I will not be able to help you now."

"This story is not yet played out. We all have our highs and our lows," said Amos. "And we look ahead, beyond the present moment. I think, Great One, my king and I would rather bet our stakes on you than on the man who sailed down the Nile this morning."

Great One. It was the first time Amos had ever called him that.

The little train set forth. Three humble travelers, a donkey and a goat. The moon looked down—Thoth, the left eye of the great sky hawk. Only Thoth knew what the future held for them. Thoth must lead them on their way.

There was no question of taking passage on a boat. They did not dare go near the docks. They must go to the north gate of the city. They must pray that there would be no questions.

Not far from the great wall, Amos went on ahead to see what they would have to face, while the others took shelter in a deserted court.

The news he brought back was bad. The worst.
"They have reinforced the guard. Three soldiers from
the temple. They are holding a torch up to each person's face. Several Kushite men are being held for
questioning."

"They'll have my description," said Taharka. "We
can't go through here."

"All the gates will be blocked," said Amos. "And
we have no time to wander about the city looking
for a way out. No, it is here or nowhere. Think,
Talos! Think, Haru!"

They thought. Then Talos spoke.

"We have a story. It is told by our bards. A band
of men was trapped inside a cave by a one-eyed
giant. Their leader put out the giant's eye and the
men clung beneath the sheep as they filed out, so he
could not feel them on their backs."

"You are saying we should rush them and put out
their eyes?" said Amos impatiently.

"No, but look." Talos gestured toward Hermes with
his burden of sacks. "If a man could hang on beneath
with his legs and arms, he would be completely hidden."

Taharka looked at him. He couldn't believe what
he was hearing.

But Amos was saying, as if he took the idea seri-
ously, "We can't all hang on under Hermes. And they
will have my description too, maybe even yours."

"They will be looking for a man and a Kushite
boy—most especially a Kushite boy. They can't arrest

every Syrian merchant who passes through the gate. As for me, I am unusual to say the least. But we must chance it that I have not been thought important."

"I think Shabataka and the sun priest will leave little to chance," said Amos grimly. "Let me think. Wait! A blue-eyed trader is unusual. A blue-eyed slave is not so unusual. And as for the skin—" he scooped up a handful of the packed earth of the courtyard. He smeared it over Talos's face, neck and arms. "The legs too. And this." He rummaged in his pack and found a square of colored cloth which he wrapped around Talos's head. "Always come prepared." He lifted his pack and dropped it onto Talos's back along with Talos's own. "There you are. A very dirty, dusty slave whose hair and skin might be any color. Who among these Nile people ever look at a slave, anyway? But, just to be safe, keep your eyes on the ground."

Weighted down by the packs, Talos didn't have much choice.

"And now," said Amos, "for the Kushite boy."

Taharka looked warily at Hermes. Talos quieted the animal saying, "Good Hermes. Good boy. Don't bray or kick."

Taharka dropped to his knees. Then he rose again. "No," he said. "I can't do it."

"You're right," said Amos. Taharka even thought he was laughing a little.

"But Hermes is a very obedient donkey, very quiet and mild." Talos sounded insulted.

"Nevertheless," said Amos.

He loosened the pack straps and removed one of the sacks from Hermes' back.

"What are you doing?" hissed Talos.

Amos emptied the sack into the court.

"My soft goods! My woolens from Corinth!"

"Someone will be very pleased," said Amos. "But we carry a more precious burden. Into the sack, young Hawk."

Hermes was indeed a very mild and obedient donkey and he did little more than startle and utter some protesting snorts and mutterings as the strange burden was hoisted up and strapped into place. He neither brayed nor kicked.

Taharka, bound and secure against Hermes' well padded ribs, had never been so outraged or so uncomfortable.

"I can't do this for long," he croaked.

"As long as you have to," said Amos. "Come. Let's go. Pray to my God. He seems to be fond of escapes from Egypt."

Talos tugged at Hermes' lead strap. Hermes balked and groaned. Taharka heard a mighty slap and was jolted past bearing as the animal set out at a trot. He soon settled down, however, and the jolting changed to swaying. Taharka thought he would be sick.

"We're in luck," he heard Amos whisper. "They're shooting dice."

The four men were, in fact, very bored with their task and had gotten interested in their game. They were not in the least suspicious of the Syrian trader with his donkey, his goat and his slave. They had had three Syrian merchants already that night.

"Where are you bound?" one of them asked, more out of curiosity than anything else.

"Not far," said Amos. "Coptos. Pottery, cloths, copperware."

"Have a good trip," said the soldier.

And so, strapped to the side of a donkey, Pharaoh was carried out of his city.

In the chamber of the god, Shabataka took possession of Taharka's cedarwood chair. He was very tired. He closed his eyes, stretched his legs, hung back his head.

But this would not do. There was no time to rest. The high priest would be here soon. So much to be settled before he left with the army, and the army must leave in two days' time.

The high priest came in on his knees with warm words of welcome. Shabataka cut them short.

"The marriage?"

"All preparations have been made, Great God. The ceremony can take place tomorrow."

"It *must* take place tomorrow. And be ready to record my name in your books immediately after, and have them begin the inscriptions on the Temple wall. From the day of my father's death. Remember.

"You will go with the army, Great One?"

"Of course." Shabataka flashed a warning glance at the kneeling man. The high priest made no protest.

"Your Companion, my lord?"

"I have brought my cousin, Tanut. He's slow in his wits, but he can perform the rites. The rest I can leave to you."

The high priest nodded. He had no objection to that!

There was a short silence. Shabataka turned his head toward the windows.

"The pretender?" he said at last.

"The city is being searched. All the gates are guarded. He will be found, Great One." The priest hesitated. "When he is found—what then?"

There was a longer silence.

"I don't know," said Shabataka. "I don't want him harmed. Not yet."

The high priest looked up in surprise. Shabataka frowned.

"Something troubles you?"

"I had thought, my lord—I had thought, when—"

"When what?"

"When Pharaoh's—when the pretender's food taster died—"

"*What?*"

And the high priest saw that the new god really was as astounded as he himself had been. He was completely confused.

As for Shabataka, after the first shock he almost

laughed out loud. He was going to like Thebes. They
weren't afraid of anything here. They had really tried
to kill him! It would have solved his problem for him.
Nevertheless—

"I don't want him harmed. Keep him close till I
return."

And he thought: the Assyrians, not the priests,
might have attempted the murder. A delaying tactic,
to keep Egypt busy with her own calamities. They
must really be on the move. And who in the Great
House was being paid by *them*? No, this war must be
fought quickly. Two days? The army must leave tomorrow.

He rose to his feet.

"Our plans have changed, high priest."

"Which plans, Great One?" The high priest felt
as if he had been running. He was not even familiar
yet with the old plans! He thanked the gods that he
was being left with the slow-witted cousin.

"The marriage will not take place tomorrow. There
is no time. When I return, they can have as big a
show as they like."

To his surprise, the high priest looked relieved.

"This pleases you?"

"Well, Holy One, there was a problem."

"What problem?"

"The divine priestess Shepnuset."

Shepnu. Little princess high-and-mighty. Little
brat. She had always been a problem.

"In fact," said the high priest, "she has locked herself up."

"That's no problem."

"In fact," the priest said again, "she has barricaded herself in."

"And you have no one who can take care of that?"

"Well, we might have some trouble finding some-body who would be willing to do it. You see—" he seemed to have some difficulty with the words. "You see, she has barricaded herself into the Holy of Holies."

For just a moment even Shabataka's skin crept. Then he really did burst out laughing.

But he sobered quickly. There was one thing on which his mind was set.

"One thing, High Priest, one thing most impor-tant. Custom or no custom, marriage or no marriage. Tomorrow you will have my name recorded in the books. Tomorrow you will begin the inscriptions on the wall. Remember. From the day of my father's death."

≈ 14 ≈

No Ships to the East

ONCE OUT of the city, beyond the reach of the temple guards, they were able to take passage on a boat. It was a freighter, the main boat towing a kind of barge loaded with fruit. They paid in barley. For an extra amount, they were allowed to fit Hermes in on the cargo barge. For food, on the evening stopovers, they caught their own fish, cooking them in a little kitchen cabin, and eating bread and beans from the sacks. Taharka no longer even thought about the tabus.

Jerusalem. The tough little city of Hezekiah. That, said Amos, was their destination. Talos didn't understand why.

"Why not settle down right here in Egypt? It's as good a place as any, till things blow over at least."

"And if they don't? Our young Hawk here is the true king of the Two Lands. The men who have risen against him can't let him go loose. Once Thebes has been searched and searched again, no place in Egypt or Kush will be safe for him. He will live as a fugitive in his own country till he is hunted down."

"And in Jerusalem, he will be safe?"

After a pause, Amos said, "There are different kinds of danger." And, to Taharka, "My king is a just man, an honorable man. He will help you. You will be king again, young Hawk."

"Neither of you will ever get out of Jerusalem alive," said Talos soberly. "I know."

"That," said Amos, "remains to be seen."

King again, thought Taharka. He had never wanted to be king, but it had happened. Was it the will of the gods? Surely Shabataka was not their will.

Shabataka.

Shepnuset.

The river flowed on between green fields with the endless cliffs of Egypt rising above the river valley. Geese, ducks, ibis, heron. The water was full of boats—sails and oars, cargo boats and pleasure boats, a yacht with a cabin and its own kitchen boat in tow, pilgrims on their way to the shrine of Osiris, god of the dead. People, just people. He was one of them now.

There were other people too, the people on the banks, the men at the water wheels, endlessly churning the river water into the fields, with no reward but what was left over from the tables of the god and his princes.

On the dock of a small town where they had tied up for the night, a farmer had been thrown down and was being beaten by a man with the look of an official.

Taharka instinctively picked up a stave used for poling out small boats and, balancing it on the palms of his hands, stepped forward and faced the attacker.

"What's the offense, friend?" he jerked his head toward the man on the stones. "I don't see a stick in *his* hands."

"Don't interfere!" said an officious voice from the crowd that had gathered. "This is the vizier's tax collector. The man has defaulted on the god's share of the grain."

"It's a lie!" shouted a small boy, his face wet with tears. "Our barley is already in the god's granary, and they only left us enough to get through the dry time. Now he wants that, too!"

The tax collector turned on the boy with his cudgel. Taharka sprang forward and deflected the blow.

There was a long sigh from the onlookers. Two men from the granary police came forward, swords drawn. But the crowd was gathering close, and the police did not seem too eager.

Taharka was remembering the days of his judgments. He remembered, long ago in Napata, the man sentenced to lose his hand.

"So you want that grain too?" he said. "For the god? Or for yourself?"

"He wants it for himself!"

"Bloodsucker! My youngest child is crippled from hunger because of him!"

The crowd was clamoring now. Everyone seemed to have his story. The three men were backing away. Now it was Taharka who was advancing, crouching like a panther.

"You know the punishment for misuse of the god's grain? Do you know—"

He felt Amos's hand on his shoulder, heard him whisper in his ear.

"Easy, Hawk. Watch your tongue."

The tax collector decided to give it up. He and his guards had a hard time getting back through the crowd. They heard him shouting:

"This will be reported! The god is not to be defied! You'll hear from us!"

"We won't," muttered Amos. "But it would be wise to stay out of sight here. Back on the boat till morning."

As they ate their bread beneath the passengers' awning, Talos said sadly:

"You're right. Egypt is not safe for our Hawk. There is no way he is going to be able to keep himself hidden."

Taharka was not hungry.

"How can these things happen? Who are the men who let these things happen?"

"A king could find out," said Amos. "I wonder if Shabataka would concern himself?"

Tanis! The great city of the Delta, so close to the vast Sea of the North. Taharka thought he could smell the salt. The Delta itself was a strange and wonderful world to him—the little fingers of the Nile spreading out and reaching to the sea, the swamps and marshes, the tall reeds and the papyrus, the little boats of the fowlers, the great green plain around the city.

Amos gazed about him with a strange, almost a remembering look.

"It was here," he said, "that my people settled when our father Jacob led them from the east. It was here that they were held captive by Pharaoh till Moses the prince led them out of slavery."

But at Tanis there was bad news.

There were no sea-going ships, no Byblos travelers tied up at the docks. Amos questioned the foreman of the dock workers.

"No sea travel now to the east," said the man. "Nothing till who knows when. Business is going to be very bad."

"Why not? What has happened?" But Amos looked as though he already knew the answer.

"A caravan came in three days ago. There's a war going on! Very heavy fighting in the cities on the eastern coast."

Amos closed his eyes.

"It has begun."

The man looked at them curiously.

"Why are you so anxious to get into it?"

"It's my home," said Amos.

"Theirs too?" said the man looking from Talos to Taharka. He seemed suspicious.

"Come," said Amos, and drew the other two away from the foreman. He whispered to Taharka.

"We must get away. Even this man wonders about us and it won't be long before patrols are posted at the borders."

"What can we do?"

"Hey!"

The foreman was calling after them. They stopped, uncertain what it meant.

But the man was not unfriendly.

"That caravan, they're as crazy as you are. They're going back. Well, we all have to earn a living."

Amos waved his thanks to the foreman.

"It's our only chance," he whispered.

They discovered that the caravan had been gathered from a Bedouin tribe known as the Mucri, who had long had close ties to Egypt. They were among the very few who now made the regular crossing across the old desert trade route from Gaza to the Egyptian frontier.

They were real desert people, the first Taharka had ever seen, lean and brown and bearded, like bright birds of prey in their big, striped robes and the head wear that protected them from the sun.

The caravan itself, camped outside the city, was like a small army. A circle of black tents guarded the animals that provided them with food and clothing. Inside the circle, the women and children went about their business, milking the goats, shaping the leather jars that formed a large part of their trade, cooking up the mutton in their big stew pots. Outside rode the armed men who guarded the camp, always watchful, for in times like these you never knew.

They had horses and donkeys. And camels! Taharka had heard of these creatures, huge and humped and ugly, traveling the desert for days without food or water. He stared at them, fascinated. What we in Kush could do with camels! he thought. We could move out, west from the river, build cities in the desert, as far as the coast of that boundless western sea, where they say the rivers run with gold—

"Stay away from them," Amos was saying. "They're mean beasts."

The chief of the clan received them in his tent. They sat cross-legged on cushions and, their hearts sinking, watched him slowly shake his head.

"We can take on no one else. You have never crossed the desert before? Then you cannot know how needful it is that we conserve our supplies. You haven't enough to sustain you. What you offer in payment is no good to us, we have our own trade goods. No, you must find another way. Or stay here and be safe. Things are bad in the east—though," he added pompously, "we of the Mucri have no fear of the Assyrians."

There was an odd sound from Talos, like a smothered sneeze.

There was another sound, too, from a curtained section of the big tent. A child was crying, a fretful, wailing cry. The chief turned his head, his face suddenly tense and anxious.

"Someone is sick?"

"It's nothing," said the chief. "We have our little ailments. My son is strong, a Mucri boy. He will be able to travel."

"He's crying from pain," said Taharka. "The little boy is suffering. Maybe I can help." The chief looked doubtful and Taharka, a little carried away, added, "I am a physician."

Amos said hastily, "He was assistant to a physician in Thebes."

Thebes. The chief was impressed.

"You may look at him if you like."

The child lay on a pile of brightly dyed sheepskins, turning his head restlessly from side to side. Taharka laid his hand on the boy's forehead. It was very hot. Looking up at the tall, black boy, not so very much older than he was, the child quieted a little.

Taharka turned the curly head to one side. The skin around the ear was red and swollen. He looked beneath. A boil. A very large boil.

Taharka let out his breath in a long sigh.

"I think I know what to do."

Talos muttered in his ear, "Are you crazy? What if something happens to him? What if they blame us?"

"I'll need figs, chopped very fine. And a grain mash. And hot water."

The ingredients were brought. Taharka set to work mixing a poultice.

"You really know what you're doing?" Amos whispered nervously.

"Well, actually I only saw Baku use it on an animal. But if it would cure a horse, why not a human? Besides, the little boy is in pain. Someone has to do something!"

"I will pray," said Amos. He went outside and covered his head.

Very carefully, Taharka applied the poultice to the boil. The boy cried out once at the hot water, then, at Taharka's soothing touch, lay still.

The chief followed the young physician into the outer tent. Taharka began his instructions as to how to apply the medicine.

"*We* will not be doing this," said the chief. "*You* will. You will stay here till I see for myself what comes of it all."

His voice was menacing. His eyes were as hard as stone.

"You see?" whispered Talos. "What did I tell you? It will be a long day before I see home again."

In any case, it was a long night. The little boy was restless. Taharka changed the poultice often, and sat by the sheepskin bed to watch his progress. Once, to sooth him to sleep, he told him a story—the story of a prince who had rescued a slave from a fabulous monster. Finally he fell asleep himself.

He woke to find the sheepskins empty. Frightened, he pushed back the curtains. The outer tent was empty too; but in the open, the air was full of a great commotion, sheep bleating, donkeys braying, horses neighing, the shrill chatter of children, the shouted commands of soldiers and camel drivers. The caravan was pulling up stakes, folding its tents, ready to go.

Bewildered, Taharka stood in the flap of the chief's tent, the soft wind of the Delta ruffling his cotton cloak. He heard Amos shouting.

"Get your things together! They've taken us on! We're moving out!"

A little boy in a brilliant red and blue robe ran to him and threw his arms around his waist.

"You can travel with me. You can be my doctor and tell me stories."

"You're well!" Taharka couldn't believe it. Had *he* done this?

"Yes," said Amos, "one way or the other, our patient recovered during the night. Look at him run! The father is full of gratitude, says we can share in their meat and their water all the way to Gaza." He paused, looking at Taharka with respect. "I owe you my thanks, Haru."

"Save your thanks," said Talos. "See if he deserves it when you get to Jerusalem. *If* you get to Jerusalem."

It was as if the breeze had suddenly turned cold.

"We?" said Amos. "You're not coming with us?"

Talos shook his head.

"I have seen the Assyrians. I will not see them again. And I tell you, Amos, it would be better for you to go alone into the desert of the west, without water, than to go where you are going."

After a long pause, Taharka said, "What will you do?"

"Settle down a while in Tanis," said Talos. "It's a pleasant town. I have enough left to make a start. I make you a present. Hermes, to carry your burdens. No, no, you will need him." He looked around him. "What a world, these cities on the Nile! Your columns, your carvings in stone! Your sciences, your medicines! We are like children there," he gestured northward, "across the sea. But we will learn."

He laid his hands on Taharka's shoulders.

"I will miss you, Great One. I am happy to have been of help to you. I am sorry for what lies ahead." He sighed. "You were learning to live in this world. You'd have made a physician. You'd have made a good man."

"He *will* make a good king," said Amos softly.

Little knots of the people of Tanis—idlers, the inquisitive, people looking for last-minute bargains—had gathered on the outskirts of the Bedouin encampment. They watched in curiosity as the caravan moved out.

Looking back, Taharka saw a man step out from

the crowd. He saw him raise his arm in a gesture of farewell.

He thought his eyes were playing tricks with him. It was the man he had collided with in the street. It was the man with the scar.

❧ 15 ❧

Shabataka in the Night

THERE WAS only one thing Taharka could say about the desert: It was hot. Even he, a son of Kush, could believe he had never felt heat before. His face and body streamed with sweat, his eyes burned with the everlasting sun. The sun—an ominous red light in the morning, rising into a great ball of fire. Then at night the same burning ball sinking in the west, followed by the cold. At night, even wrapped in one of the Bedouins' woolen robes, he shivered.

The crossing, said the chief, took ten days. One day seemed like a year.

Their water was running low and poor Hermes was suffering greatly when they finally came to a well. The well, a little spot of green shaded by date palms, was guarded by armed men. "In the old days," said the chief, "these waters were guarded by soldiers from Egypt. Now they are our wells, Mucri wells. If anyone tries to steal our water, we kill him."

"What if he is dying of thirst?" said Taharka.

"One way or the other, he dies," said the chief shortly.

Then on again, on and on across the sand. None of it seemed to bother Taharka's little patient or the other children. They knew, as if they were born to it—which of course they were—how to save their strength, hunker down beneath their cotton robes, trudge along with their eyes to the ground, wordless and without complaint. Then, when the sun went down, they raced about like young animals let loose from a cage.

Amos, too, seemed to take it all in stride. Wrapped in his robe and head cloth, as brown as the Mucri, he might have been one of them. Silent and stolid, handling his stave like a Bedouin, he might have lived his life among the tents and pack animals of the sands.

"It's in the blood," he said, as they sat by the stew pot, reaching in for the big chunks of meat. "My people were desert people once. Forty years, they wandered in the wilderness, never coming to shelter in a town or a city, driven away from the water holes and the caravan routes."

"How did they live?" Taharka wondered if he could live out the ten days' crossing.

"They managed. They fought for their wells. And our God Jahveh from the mountain sent down bread from heaven, lying in flakes on the ground, to be gathered each day at dawn, enough for every person. They called it manna."

"What else did they eat?"

Little Sabi, the chief's son had come over for another story.

"Well," said Amos, "God sent quails up from Kush to the Northern Sea and they stopped to rest a while in the desert. They were very tired, and my people were able to catch them by hand and eat them."

"And water? Before they had fought for their wells?"

"Not far from the wells of Rephidim," said Amos, "is a wall of rock with water seeping through. Jahveh from the Mountain told Moses what to do. Moses struck through the crust, the water poured out in streams and the people drank and watered their beasts. So they were refreshed and strengthened, and were able to fight and win against the men who would have driven them from the wells and let them die of thirst."

Sabi looked thoughtful at the last part. He gave a sudden, determined nod of his head.

"I don't think," he said, "that I will ever let anyone die of thirst."

At the second well, Hermes collapsed. He was not a Bedouin donkey. He was a donkey of the Nile, used to green reeds and plenty of water and shelter from the sun. Amos and Taharka, with help from

Sabi, were able to drag him into the shade of a date palm.

"Don't concern yourselves," said the chief generously. "The desert is full of the bones of donkeys. You can load your belongings—they're light enough —on one of our camels."

"No!" said Taharka.

This was Talos's donkey, Talos's gift to them, and Talos had been fond of it. Besides, he owed the animal a debt—probably his life.

"We must soak a cloth in cool water and cover his head. We must keep it soaked. We must keep him cool."

"Water? Our precious water?" The chief's face was dark with outrage.

"And we must wait till he recovers. He will die if he moves out."

"*You* will wait till he recovers. *We* move out when our water skins are full."

Sabi stood up to face his father.

"*I* will wait till he recovers. This is Haru's donkey. Haru saved my life."

Taharka thought that this was putting it a little strongly, but he did not contradict him.

Sabi was the only one of the Mucri who had ever been able to out-stare the chief. He could do it every time. The chief lowered his eyes and shrugged.

"One night," he said. "We will wait one night. There were things that can be attended to here as well as anywhere. Let us pray the beast is dead in the morning."

"He won't be dead," said Sabi when they were alone. He looked thoughtfully at the older boy. "The way you spoke to my father. No one speaks to him that way. It was as if you were a chief, too." Then he added, approvingly, "And Hermes is a royal donkey."

Taharka looked at Hermes, surprised. Now that he thought about it, even lying there gasping, Hermes did have a princely look—sleek, slender, silvery gray, a real Nile donkey. Talos had made them a princely gift. He missed Talos. He wrung out the cloth and laid it on Hermes' head.

Hermes was not dead in the morning. He had, in fact, struggled to his feet during the night and was trotting happily about, munching the thorn bushes. Puzzled but relieved, Taharka and Amos prepared to load him with their two small packs. Hermes balked, reared and kicked, letting out what was almost a roar of protest.

"He's telling you he's sick!" said Sabi indignantly. "He can't carry packs."

Amos and Taharka looked at each other and then at Hermes, who looked back with an expression of smug suffering.

"I don't believe this," said Taharka.

"I believe it," said Amos. "I think he did it on purpose."

The chief did not repeat the offer of a camel and the refugees from Thebes ended by carrying their packs themselves till he finally relented. Hermes, meanwhile, picked his way gracefully over the sand, free of burdens, truly a royal donkey.

Then one night—Taharka heard it in the dark, swelling from a whisper to a roar—came the sound of chariot wheels, rolling and rattling, and then the endless rhythm of running feet, running to the beat of the dogged Kushite chant.

"Hey ho, hey ho, Pha-raoh, Pha-raoh—"

Shabataka's army was passing them in the night.

He stood in the flap of the tent. He could see nothing but dust with the starlight filtering through.

Amos stood behind him.

"He's wasting no time," he said.

"No. He's running them in the dark to beat the heat of the sun."

The voices in the night, the throb of the running feet had died away. The earth was still again.

The anger rose inside Taharka in a sickening wave.

"I hate him. Someday I will bring him down."

"And re-claim your kingdom? That will be difficult."

Difficult? Impossible. By now Shabataka was confirmed, listed in the books of the priests, married to Shepnuset—

"Shepnu! Why didn't she come with me?"

For a moment Amos said nothing. Then:

"Sometimes you are born to—or are given—duties you can't escape."

His voice was tired, full of a strange sadness. But Taharka didn't notice. He was absorbed in his own pain.

"She was my best friend, the only girl I'll ever really love. Shabataka! He never even liked her."

"Listen," said Amos gently. "Don't be too sure of all that has happened. She is very tough. And she is Priestess. The real ruler in Thebes."

For some reason, Taharka wanted to hurt him.

"You don't understand. You don't have a wife or children. You never loved anyone—"

"Why do you say that? I loved someone once."

Taharka looked at him, distracted for a moment. He had never really thought of Amos as someone with a life and feelings of his own. He was just the messenger, the goad, intent on whatever was best for his king.

But he was also someone else, the man he had somehow known he could trust, that terrible night in Thebes.

"It was a long time ago," said Amos. "I was just a little older than you are now. She lived in a village on the border where the Assyrians patrolled. They had had an order for laborers in the north, and they couldn't fill it, so they crossed over and took away the village. The whole village. All of them. I never saw her again."

The look in his eyes was one of terrible grief. And more.

"I wasn't there. I should have been there. If I had been there—"

So that was the reason for that constant fire in Amos's eyes. That was the duty he couldn't escape. "No time, no time." He must act, he must never give up, he must make up for what he hadn't done that long-ago day on the border.

"If you had been there, what?" said Taharka. "What would you have done?" He shook his head. "If they want something they take it, people like that. They don't even think about it."

Men like this Sennacherib.

Men like Shabataka.

"I will bring him down. Somehow."

And then what?

Terrible thoughts rose in his mind. It was hard for him to speak them aloud.

"In the old days of Kush, if a king was to be killed they didn't shed his blood. That was tabu. They strangled him, or walled him up alive, or—"

Amos's hand was on his shoulder, steadying him, drawing him back.

"Don't think of these things now. Go back to sleep. We need all our strength for what lies ahead."

🌿 16 🌿

The Sea and the Smoke

SOMETHING strange had happened. There had been a trembling in the earth.

"And did you see the shadow in front of the tent?" said Amos. "It has moved back." There was a tremor in his voice. "It moved back! The sun itself moved back!" The sun had moved back from west to east. Time itself had moved back . . . Not far, just a little, but it had *moved.* It couldn't be, but it was. What did it mean? Was it an omen? What did it foretell? Was it for good or ill?

Amos thought he knew. The awe in his voice turned to excitement. "Beware, O Assyrians! Jahveh is still in his heavens!"

The desert crossing was over. They had come to the walled city of Gaza.

But Gaza would not let them in.

"You're trouble," they were told by a guard. "You are under the curse of the Almighty."

124

"What almighty?" The chief was indignant. "We are faithful servants of the Baals. The Baals have never cursed us."

"Not Baal!" The guard made the sign against evil. "The king. The Great King."

"What king?"

"The king from the north. Sennacherib the Almighty."

The chief spat on the ground.

After a moment's stunned silence, the guard cried out in horror.

"Get out! Get your cheap stuff out of here! You're not getting us in trouble with the Assyrians!"

Cheap stuff! Taharka was as angry as if he himself had been insulted. There were goods from the Nile in the Mucri packs, expensive Egyptian pottery, fine cloths from Kush, jewelry of gold and turquoise mined in the desert.

Some of the younger Mucri spearmen wanted to fight. But the chief knew it was no use. Gaza was a big town of the Philistines, well guarded by its militia. The little caravan wouldn't stand a chance.

"Something has happened. They never kept us out before. We will move on to Askelon. It's only a half day's journey. May the Baals protect us from what we may find there."

The desert was behind them. They had come to a narrow green strip of coastal land with fig trees and mulberries, olive groves and fields of wheat and barley. The ground was covered with scarlet and blue flowers. Taharka had never seen such a land—and no river, no Father Nile to water it and keep it green. What a wonder!

"We are past the time of the winter rains," said Amos, "or you would soon see why we have no need of Father Nile!"

Water from heaven. As in the forests Embutah had told him of, the forests of his birth. Taharka wished that he could see it.

And, as they drew closer to the coast, he really could smell salt on the breeze from the west.

"The sea?" he said.

"When we come to Askalon," said Amos, "you can see it."

But suddenly Taharka felt that he could not wait till they came to Askalon. A kind of mad impatience rose up within him; and, before he himself knew just what he was going to do, he had jumped onto Hermes' back and trotted off from the caravan, straight to the west. He was guided by the smell of the salt and then by a strange sound, like nothing he had ever heard before. The surging of the sea. The soft roll of waters.

And suddenly there it was!

Water—endless, out to the horizon, blue and glinting sparkles of gold beneath the sun.

The end of the world, thought Taharka, filled with awe. Nothing out there. Nothing ever again but water. What ship would venture out beyond that short white line of surf, on and on, to who knew where or what?

And yet he knew it was not the end of the world. There were ships that ventured out. It led to Talos' land and unimaginable places beyond—places where white rain fell and savage people kept themselves warm with the skins of beasts—

He was dreaming. The water had drawn him into a kind of sleep. He blinked and shook himself awake. He must ride back to meet the caravan. He wished he could stay forever, lulled and enchanted by that vast, monotonous blue and that strange, restless, never-ending sound.

What was that in the air?

Not the salt, not the sea. This was something new, a strange, heavy smell, faint but foul. Smoke? Had he imagined it, or was it getting heavier?

I must get back quickly, he thought. But at least I have seen it. Once in my life I have seen the sea.

The caravan never reached Askalon. The smoke in the air hung heavy now. What lay before them had come to meet them.

One moment the horizon lay before them, clear and green. The next, as in Talos' story, it was black with men and horses, blotting out the sun.

And for the first time, Taharka saw them. The Assyrians.

❧ 17 ☙

Rab Shaka

"YOU ARE MUCRI?" A man looked down on them from a high chariot with cruel iron blades on the spokes of its heavy wheels. His face, half covered by a curling black beard, was as hard and cruel as the iron, with narrow, squinting eyes, the corners lined from the sun. His body shirt of shining metal scales gave him the look of some great reptile. He spoke the language of the Babylonians, which Taharka had learned, but his accent was strange, back-country and harsh.

The Bedouins whispered among themselves—was this the king? But Taharka, who had been Pharaoh, knew otherwise. An important man, no doubt, but not the king.

"We are the Mucri," the chief said proudly. He too, as a trader, understood the languages of the northeast, but he answered defiantly in his own.

The Assyrian laughed, a grim, grating laugh.

"You may well be the Mucri, the last of your breed. Your little army of sand ramblers, stirred up by the accursed Egyptians, is destroyed, not far from Askalon. And, in case you wonder about the smoke, that is Askalon itself.

The chief did not lower his eyes, but the muscles of his face tightened. His brother had been in the little army of "sand ramblers."

"Who is this?"

The shrewd little eyes of the Assyrian had shifted to the face of the tall, black youth from Kush. Taharka met their scrutiny with all the pride he could muster. He could do no less than the Bedouin chief.

"He is not Mucri," said the soldier.

"He is called Hawk. He is our physician."

"Hawk?" The Assyrian turned to his men with a shout of laughter. Obediently, they echoed his mirth. "And physician? Shouldn't he still be playing doctor in the children's yard?"

"For you, sir," said Taharka softly, "I would prescribe less wine. Your nose is very red."

The air was very still. The Assyrian was no longer laughing. He leaned forward from the chariot, his eyes like slits. Taharka did not flinch, but all his flesh felt cold. The smell of the smoke from Askalon was stronger now. A second chariot had come up beside the first. Its rider, backed by his driver and two shield men, was respectful but impatient.

"Time is growing short, my lord the Tartan. We must move out quickly to join the king at Lachish. What about these?" He jerked his hand toward the caravan. "Shall I bring out the executioners?"

Taharka, even in that moment, noticed that no one in the caravan cried out, not even the children. The Tartan—he dimly remembered that this was the title of the general of the armies—did not move. At last he spoke.

"No. They can be useful." He looked again at Taharka—a hard appraising look. "Bring them with us to Lachish. Let them see for themselves what becomes of those who rebel against us."

The caravan, surrounded by Assyrian horsemen—so they really did use mounted soldiers!—was marched eastward across the plain. Before them stretched the long, blue line of the mountains of Judah. The sight of them sent a bitter loneliness shooting through Taharka. He had failed, he told himself. He had never reached his refuge in Jerusalem, never found help against his enemies, never even had a chance to fight. Had the world failed, too, and the gods? Was there no help against these powers of evil?

On high ground at the edge of the hill country stood the walled fortress town of Lachish. Far off, they could hear the voices, first a low drone as of bees in the distance, then louder and louder till it had swelled to a roar. And Taharka felt as if his heart had left him.

For, camped below the walls of Lachish, was the main army of the Assyrians. The ground was black with them, swarmed with them. Soon they were surrounded by them, the noise of the camp all around them. Horses and pack animals neighed and brayed, almost drowning the din of their human masters. Taharka looked around him, trying to catch his breath. There were the chariots, the high chariots of the Assyrians, sheathed and spiked with iron. And there they were, what Talos had told him of, the towers on wheels, the mighty armored siege engines of Sennacherib's army, lined up in wall-like rows, the great jagged rams jutting out beyond. Gangs of men were laboring with spades and picks and axes and mallets, throwing up ramps to the wall, the ramps over which those awesome machines would roll.

Lachish was circled with the black tents of the Assyrians—tents for the captains, tents for supplies and equipment, and one great tent of many colors rising above them all. All eyes in the caravan were drawn to it. They could not look away. They knew, with no question at all, whose tent that was—the royal tabernacle of Sennacherib the King.

A man had come out of that tabernacle, flanked by two spearmen. The soldiers stood back from him as he made his way toward the caravan.

"The Rab Shaka!" their guards were shouting. "Show respect!"

The Rab Shaka was spokesman and cup bearer to the king. Even the Tartan, coming forth to greet him, showed respect. The two men—the rough, sun-darkened Tartan, and the pale, mild-mannered Rab Shaka—talked together in low tones.

The Rab Shaka seemed surprised by the presence of the caravan. He moved among them, scanning their faces, one by one.

"Mucri," he said at last. "Do you know what has become of your army?"

The Bedouins were silent.

"You know. But you did not see them die."

Silence still. Only one very small boy had begun to cry.

"It was wise to bring you here," said the spokesman gravely. "Now you can see for yourselves."

He had come to Taharka. He smiled and shook his head.

"A Kushite. Yes, we know who is behind this rebellion. Well, they have had a lesson. A harsh one. They won't trouble us for a while."

So Shabataka's army had been defeated. He was beginning to understand why. Talos' stories didn't really do justice to the Assyrians.

The Rab Shaka's eyes had narrowed.

"But you are not a trader's boy."

"They say he is their 'physician'," snorted the Tartan.

The Rab Shaka looked at Taharka a long time. Then he turned away. He nodded to the Tartan.

Under strict guard, the Bedouins were allowed to build their fires and cook their food. Amos and Taharka ate little, and in silence. They had no heart for conversation.

"Will they kill us?" said Taharka at last.

"They haven't done it yet. Hold on to that."

"Amos. Haru."

A shadow had fallen across the light from the camp fire. It was Sabi. He was carrying his mutton and beans.

"Can I eat with you?"

They made room for him. Sabi, too, was very quiet; but, when he spoke, his voice was steady.

"Is this our last night?"

"I don't think so," said Amos gently. "I think they want us to see a terrible thing tomorrow, and spread the word among the tribes. Don't be afraid, Sabi."

"I'm not afraid!" Then, ashamed but honest, the little boy lowered his head. "Yes, I am afraid. I'm afraid of that man."

"The Tartan?"

"Not the Tartan," said Sabi scornfully. "He reminds me of my Uncle Omri. It's the other one, the one with the rings and the earrings. He's the bad one."

"You're a good judge of people, Sabi," said Amos approvingly. "You'll make a wise chief."

"He was looking at Hermes, Haru," said Sabi suddenly. "I think he wants him."

"Hermes?" Taharka was startled. Hermes was the last thing on his mind.

"You know the Nile donkeys are better than the ones from the east," said Sabi reasonably. "They price them almost as high as a good horse." He added bitterly, "I would hate for the Assyrians to have Hermes."

So would Talos, thought Taharka. For that matter, he would hate it himself.

"Well, Sabi," he said. "We must see to it that the Assyrians don't get Hermes."

For the first time, Sabi smiled.

"Do they have princes in Kush?" he asked.

Taharka laughed. "Kush is crawling with princes!"

"I think," said Sabi, "you must be one of them. Only you're not the kind that crawls."

The shadow across the fire light was bigger this time. An Assyrian spearman in his serpent-like mail shirt had arrived, half his face hidden by his short, square beard.

"The physician? The one they call Hawk?"

Slowly Taharka rose to his feet.

"Come with me. You have been summoned."

❧18❧

The Tabernacle

THE TENT was like the house of a very rich man. Rich rugs covered the ground. Rich curtains overhung alcoves the size of rooms, and soft voices hummed behind them. One was evidently a kitchen, and Taharka's mouth watered at the savory odors hanging in the air.

At the end of what looked like a great hall was a low chair, and in it a man. He was simply dressed, like a soldier at rest, but the jewels on his fingers and arms could have ransomed a city. He was slender, not very tall, not very old. His heavy, black beard was held in place by a jeweled net. His face, half turned away and outlined by the light from the clay lamps was narrow, sharp nosed, handsome. Taharka could not see his eyes.

The soldier laid his hand on Taharka's shoulder to move him forward. Taharka shook it off and walked slowly toward the man in the chair. There was no doubt in his mind who it was.

The Rab Shaka hovered over the chair. He spoke to Taharka, as if to a slave.

"On your knees before the king."

Taharka hesitated. An instant too long. The soldier thrust him to the ground with the butt end of his spear, and held him there. Taharka gritted his teeth against the pain.

"Enough."

The voice was flat, toneless, indifferent, but was instantly obeyed. The soldier took away the spear. Taharka straightened his back and raised his head. Now he could see the man's eyes. They could have been the eyes of Shabataka.

"They say you're a doctor."

"A physician's assistant." Taharka was pleased with himself. His voice was steady. He had made up his mind. He would say nothing but what was asked of him. Nothing added, nothing explained.

"There could be plenty of work for you here. The pay is good."

"The army of Sennacherib has no physicians?" Already he had broken his rule.

Sennacherib the King smiled, just a little. He leaned forward in his chair, his eyes narrowed, searching the eyes of Taharka.

"Who are you?"

"My name is Haru."

"Yes, Haru. Hawk. Not a common name among common men. *What* are you?"

"I'm a physician's assistant."

"A physician's assistant. A boy. A Kushite boy who speaks the tongue of Babylon and Nineveh in the accents of the courts, who has crossed the desert route with Bedouin rebels on his way—where? And why?"

Taharka said nothing. He did not lower his eyes. After a while, the king leaned back in his chair.

"Our scribes need information for their records. News from Egypt is confused and hard to gather. The Kushite kings still wear the double crown?"

"They do." Taharka did not try to conceal his pride. If they did not, he thought, there would be no double crown.

"*Who* wears the crown? Our recorders still write of the old king—Shaba? Shabaka? But now we hear of a Shebitku—Shabtaku—and rumors of a pretender who pops up here and there—Tarku— Tirhaka—"

"Taharka is the true king!"

Taharka himself was startled by the ring of anger in his voice. Careful, Haru, he told himself. You are Hawk, the physician's apprentice. What difference to you who wears the double crown?

The king was smiling again, his wise little smile.

"That's as may be." He stretched himself like a cat, turning his head toward the Rab Shaka. "What was the other thing? Oh, yes. The beast."

The Rab Shaka whispered in his ear.

"Worth the price of a good horse? Yes, a fine gift for my boy in Nineveh, my little Esarhaddon."

The king's face had suddenly softened. And, for some reason, Taharka felt a strange thrill along his spine like a warning of the future. He did not understand why.

But the king had finished.

"No more tonight. There's a hard day ahead of us tomorrow. You will find it interesting, young Hawk. And think, as you watch it, of Egypt and Kush."

He nodded to the Rab Shaka, who nodded to Taharka's guard. Taharka was jerked to his feet. He looked back once as he was led from the tent. The king and the Rab Shaka were talking softly. The Rab Shaka was watching him.

Sabi rose from the camp fire as they approached, wiping away the traces of tears.

"I thought we would never see you again."

"What happened?" Amos's face was tense.

Taharka glanced at Sabi and shook his head.

"They just wanted some information for their records."

"Their records!" said Amos, with contempt. "They don't need information. They write whatever will please the king, and the stonecutters engrave it on their pillars."

Sabi clung suddenly to Taharka.

"I *am* afraid, Haru," he whispered again. "I'm afraid of tomorrow."

❧ 19 ❧

"Don't Let Them See
You Cry"

"UP, UP YOU Mucri rebels! On your feet! See
what becomes of traitors! Watch and see!"

The sun was red in the east. Still heavy with
sleep, the Bedouins were herded together to witness
the death of Lachish.

The little fortress city stood tight and proud on
its high ground across the plain, surrounded by its
deep wall of heavy brick and stone. On the wall and
on the turrets the defenders of the town had massed
themselves with their bows and slings and fire sticks.
Taharka's heart beat fast with sympathy and an un-
reasonable hope. Could they do it? Could they hold
out? They were brave enough. Their walls were strong.

"The king comes forth!"

On a rise of ground above the tabernacle a throne
had been raised—a high, armed chair of cedar wood,
carved with figures of slaves and captives, draped with
rich cloth of purple from the city of Tyre. To the
sound of trumpets, the massive folds of the great tent

139

were drawn back and Sennacherib the King came out into the light.

Today he was appareled as a king indeed—a fringed purple robe embroidered and shot with silver, bracelets of heavy gold on his arms, purple boots on his feet, the high crown of Assyria on his head. His hair and beard were clubbed and netted and shone with gold and jewels. Rejecting the aid of his guards, he gathered up the skirt of his robe and hopped onto the throne, as jauntily as a boy vaulting a donkey. Once again Taharka was reminded of Shabataka with his poise and self-confidence. The air echoed with the shouts of the soldiers.

A spearman placed in his left hand the long, lithe Assyrian bow and, in his right, the iron-headed arrow. The shouts had died away. The silence was broken only by the birds who, at least, seemed to be going about business as usual.

Slowly, almost casually, Sennacherib fitted the arrow to the bow, sighting along the shaft like a man testing his weapon. He let the arrow fly. It found no mark, the king being positioned well beyond the range of the bowmen on the walls. But, as it pierced the ground below the city, a roar that shook the earth arose from the army of the Assyrians.

There was no more silence. The air shivered with the sound of bulls' horns and trumpets of brass. And then the drums. And then, thrust forward from behind by the straining, quivering men of the infantry

with their groaning cries of "Heave! Heave! Heave!"
the siege engines rolled out.

Up the earthen ramps they crawled like giant bee-
tles or warrior ants. Nothing could stop them. Arrows and rocks from the slings rained down from
the walls. The giant guard-shields turned them aside
like toys.

"The fire!" hissed Taharka, teeth clenched, shivering, as if there were a question as to how it would
all end. "Where is their fire?"

The defenders had fire—torches blazing with burning oil, fire bombs hurtling down upon the siege
cars. The air began to fill with the sickening smell of
smoke they remembered from Askelon. A scream
arose from one of the men guiding the rams. But
every tower had its supply of water, and behind every
guard-shield stood a man whose only task was to
douse the flames. The siege engines rolled on.

Sennacherib nodded to the Tartan who nodded to
the high captain of the infantry. The drums thun-
dered. The foot soldiers began to march and, flanking
them, the bowmen artillery ran on ahead, crouching
behind the shield bearers, dropping to their knees to
take aim. The first of the Lachish defenders to die
fell from the walls—slowly, it seemed, turning and
tumbling in the air. Soon the air was full of those
twisting, turning bodies, full of cries and shrieks of
agony.

"Gods! Gods!" whispered Taharka. "Why don't

they come out? Why don't they meet them on the ground?"

"Watch and see," said Amos bitterly.

The gate had been opened. The men of Lachish poured out in their peaked helmets, swords and spears at the ready. Taharka could not hear but he could see Sennacherib's laughter. With an almost good-humored gesture, he waved toward a rise of ground not far away. And down they poured at his command. Not chariots, but men on horseback. For the first time, Taharka saw what they could do. Once in his childhood days he had seen a pride of lions closing in on a gazelle. The picture burned in his mind as he watched the horsemen of Sennacherib closing in on the line of men issuing from the gate of Lachish. A few of them broke away. The horses swerved as easily, it seemed, as men on foot, but so high and terrible above the helpless foot soldiers, hooves trampling, their riders with swords already red with blood hacking down from those unassailable heights. One man managed to dodge free, running out across the field toward where the Mucri caravan stood to "watch and see." The horsemen held back a little, playing with him like cats with a mouse. Taharka thought he might make it and strained forward, his hands stretched out to draw him into the shelter of the little band. The Mucri were ready to fight for him, with sticks and stones if need be. But the horsemen tired of the game, closed upon him and cut and trampled him down.

And now the siege cars had reached the walls, the great jagged rams in place. "Heave! Heave! Heave!" Crack, crumble, crash. Bricks and earth poured inward, the giant stones groaned and tottered and fell. Great gaping holes appeared in the walls. Taharka closed his eyes. The town of Lachish was open to its enemies.

The Assyrian infantry was running now, line upon line of men, spears leveled, thirsty for blood. The soldiers of Lachish were no longer soldiers. Like small terrified animals pursued by predators they scurried here and there about the field. And the predators had no mercy. There were to be no war prisoners. Not one was to be left alive. Grim and business-like, like market butchers, the Assyrians slashed and thrust. The chariots rolled across the plain, crushing all that stood or lay in their path. And the whole great army, as if according to some inexorable plan, now drew together, bearing down upon the gaping wall of Lachish.

The sun was high. It had not taken long. The captive caravan was prodded forward, spears to their backs.

"Up, up, you Mucri, up to the wall! Watch and see!"

The horror had begun. The Assyrians poured through the breaches in the wall. Inside the city the fires had begun to burn and a great, mushroom-like cloud of black smoke rose and hung above the turrets and roof tops. The drums and the trumpets were

still and the cries of the people, one endlessly keening wail, hung in the air like the smoke.

Then Taharka saw them, beneath the wall, through
the breaches and the gateway. The sign of the Assyrians. The lifeless bodies thrust through and hanging
high upon the long, sharpened stakes.

"Stand tall, Sabi," said Taharka, for the little boy
had quailed and tried to hide his face. "Don't let
them see you cry."

And, though trembling, the little boy stood stony
still and watched the scene of terror.

After a while the lines appeared on the ramps and
the roadway—lines of women, children, young boys,
a few old men, roped together and tottering beneath
the loads of the wealth of Lachish heaped upon their
backs.

"Where are they going?" whispered Sabi. "Where
will they take them?"

"They will carry the robbers' loot as far as Nineveh,"
said Amos, "those few who survive. After that, who
knows? May God pity them, these people of Judah."

On a gold-washed litter, raised high like a god,
Sennacherib the King had been brought up too, to
"watch and see." Slowly Taharka turned to look upon
him. What would he see in his face? Pity? Regret
for "necessary severity"? Hatred for the rebels? Cruel
pleasure at their suffering?

He saw none of these. Sennacherib looked bored.
He had done a good day's work and wanted it over
quickly so he could get back to the good dinner that

awaited him in his tabernacle, perhaps dictate a letter to his favorite son, his little boy in Nineveh.

"Gods!" thought Taharka. "How I hate him!"

It was a deep and abiding hatred. And for a while he could not distinguish his hatred for Sennacherib from his hatred for his brother Shabataka.

The dead, most of the population of the little fortress town, had been hastily piled into a mass grave, a rock tomb south of the city. The smoke was drifting away. The Tartan, flanked by his guards, tired and grim, walked restlessly up and down before the Bedouin caravan.

"So, Mucri," he said, "you have seen? You have learned a good lesson? You will teach it well?"

There was no reply. The Bedouins watched him, fascinated, exhausted, stunned by the terror of the day.

"You are free to go," said the Tartan.

Dazed and stumbling, they struggled to their feet.

"All but one," said the Tartan.

Taharka closed his eyes and dropped his sack. He had known it all along.

"The Kushite boy," said the Tartan. "The 'physician.' The Great King has use for him in Jerusalem."

For a long moment he looked at Taharka, a measuring, searching look. Then he turned away.

"The rest of you," he said, "move out."

Sabi clung to Taharka.

"I won't leave you," he said. "I can't leave you here to be killed."

"They won't kill me," said Taharka. "I think they have another purpose in mind. And listen Sabi, I have a job for you." He dropped to his knees, his hands on the little boy's shoulders. "You were right. They do want Hermes. The king wants him for his son in Nineveh. Hermes is a Nile donkey, a royal donkey. He must not serve the Assyrians. You must take him quickly, hide him among the pack animals, and move out. Now."

And, as it happened, the sun was not much lower when an Assyrian soldier appeared with orders to move the "Kushite donkey" to the king's temporary stables beneath the wall of the city.

But Hermes was gone.

Taharka saw Amos once more before the Mucri caravan moved out. Amos made no offer to remain with him, but looked at him a long time, as if trying to convey a message.

"I will see you again," he said softly. "Soon. At Jerusalem."

☙ 20 ❧

"Pharaoh, King of Egypt"

HIGH ON ITS lofty plateau, surrounded by its limestone cliffs, guarded by its mountains, stood the dark little city of Jerusalem. Not very big, no river to guard it, no great fortifications, but Taharka's heart stirred strangely at the sight of it. As a child, he had heard stories. David, a mighty warrior king. A wise king, Solomon, who had married a princess of Egypt. And it was the city of Amos and—what was the king's name? Hezekiah? The king who had said "No more!" to the Assyrians.

And so now the Assyrians were here, massed before the gray walls of the city as they had been massed before the walls of Lachish. Not the whole army, that had not been thought necessary. For some time now the city had been under siege, cut off from its food supplies by the Assyrian patrols, shut in like a bird in a cage. So Sennacherib had remained in Lachish, preparing for a southward expedition to mop up what was left of the desert rebellions. The

147

Tartan commanded the Jerusalem wing. The Rab Shaka also was present.

But what puzzled Taharka most was their treatment of himself. It was, to say the least, not what he had expected of Assyrian captivity.

He sat alone in his tent. His own tent. All to himself. A servant to bring him food.

They had brought him a change of clothes. A fine tunic, a robe of embroidered cloth. The garments, he thought, of an Assyrian prince.

He didn't understand it. What was going on? He thought of the old stories of ancient god kings, pampered, served for a year, then slain in sacrifice, in honor of the gods.

But they seemed to have had something else in mind. "The King has use for you in Jerusalem," the Tartan had said.

What?

A mouse ran over his foot. The camp was overrun with them, drawn by the grain, perhaps, the left-over food from the tents of the officers. He shook himself in disgust. Then he heard steps outside.

He had a visitor.

His guard held back the flap of the tent, bowing low in respect, and into the circle of light from the earthenware lamp stepped the Rab Shaka.

Amazed and wary, Taharka rose to his feet. To his further astonishment, the Rab Shaka gently bowed his head in a gesture of courtesy between equals. He glanced around the tent.

"They have seen to your comfort?"

Taharka relaxed a little and nodded, then shook his head in wonder.

"I understand why the Assyrians take few prisoners," he said. "There would be nothing left for the king!"

"But then," said the Rab Shaka, "you are not an ordinary prisoner."

Taharka stiffened, suddenly alert. But the Rab Shaka smiled reassuringly.

"You are, after all, a—physician. A wonderful thing to be a physician. Our lives are in your hands."

"I am not a physician," said Taharka. He did not like being played with. "I am only an assistant and a student of the craft."

"Yes, a student. A student of other things as well. Languages, courtly manners—well, after all, it is your study of the physician's craft that concerns us." He seemed suddenly distracted. "There is some sickness among our men. All at once. A curious thing."

"If I can help—" said Taharka. A sick man was a sick man, Assyrian or not. It would give him something to occupy his time.

"We have physicians of our own." The Rab Shaka had tired of the game. His eyes narrowed. "But you could be of help to us. In another way."

"No other way," said Taharka sharply. "You forget, I traveled with the Mucri. I am your enemy." He thought of what he had seen at Lachish. If he never had another enemy in the world, the Assyrian would be his enemy.

"And," said the Rab Shaka, "you have watched and seen what becomes of our enemies." He was smiling, but Taharka felt for him a horror he had never known before. "On the other hand, our friends—we have many friends. Physicians. Princes." The word, and the man's sharp gaze struck the boy like a blow.

The Assyrian rose and moved restlessly about the tent.

"I put a puzzle before you. Suppose, in some foreign land, there was a prince—a prince of the royal blood—who wanted to be king. A pretender. The true king, if you like. But he was driven out by another pretender—another king—forced to take refuge with sand ramblers, the scum of the desert. And then help came to him where he least expected it. A mighty lord, a king of kings, offered him his hand in friendship—offered him his power and all his armed might to give him what he wanted."

He laughed suddenly.

"Here's another puzzle. What if this man—this boy—were not a prince at all? What if he were some runaway thief off the docks of Napata, thrown into our hands by a stroke of luck, offered a prize beyond the dreams of such a piece of scum—"

Taharka jumped to his feet. He was shaking. He had never felt such anger.

The Rab Shaka waved his hand gently.

"It's only a puzzle." He sighed and shrugged. "The

point is, it wouldn't matter. If the king of kings says a thing is so, it is so."

It was true. Such was the power of Sennacherib. Taharka's rage turned to cold despair. They don't care, he thought. They don't care who I am. King or god or beggar boy, it doesn't matter to them. The truth, the law, the gods—nothing matters to them but their greed and power.

"And what," said the Rab Shaka, "do you think my king would ask in return?"

His mouth dry, Taharka heard himself whisper: "What would he ask?"

Suddenly the Rab Shaka's manner changed. Hard and sharp, like a trader. This was an offer. This was business.

"No more resistance. Loyalty, as to an overlord. Help in time of trouble, like this. And tribute. Gold. Manpower. Stones from your mines." He was smiling again. "You see? So little, really. And in return—well, tomorrow you will see what we have in mind." Still smiling, the friendly visitor. But his eyes were like stone. "And after all, life is the greatest return of all. Whether it is the life of a man, a city or . . ." he paused, "the life of an entire land."

He rose to his feet.

"We will talk again. After tomorrow. Tomorrow I will lay the mercy of my king before this little rebel princeling in the city. We are a merciful people, you know. You have seen our righteous anger. Tomorrow you will see how merciful we can be."

Suddenly he jumped. Taharka jumped, too, his nerves as tight as a bowstring.

"Mice! Where do they come from?" He shook his robe and went out grumbling. "They're worse than the Mucri."

The Rab Shaka sat in his chair before the gray wall of Jerusalem. Behind him stood the Tartan. Behind the Tartan were ranged the elite guard of the Assyrians, tall men, straight and still, covered by their shields. And before them stood Taharka. They had brought him out, dressed in his Assyrian finery, to see and, for some reason, to be seen.

Before them all stood the crier with his voice like a trumpet of bull horn.

"Come out! Come out, Hezekiah, king of Judah. Come out and hear the words of your King of Kings."

There was a creaking sound at the great main gate. Taharka leaned forward. Was he at last to see this mad rebel against a mighty empire, this courageous prince, Amos' "glorious king?"

A man came through the gate, attended only by two scribes with tablets and writing sticks. No, it could not be the king. An elderly, bearded man in a peaked hat and fine linen robe, a man of rank and authority, but not the king. His eyes, tired and wary, looked full into the eyes of the Rab Shaka. He bowed, but only in courtesy, not as one offering tribute.

"I am Eliakim, son of Hilkiah, lord of the king's household. I will hear the words of your king."

He spoke in the court language of Babylon. The Rab Shaka smiled, a little flicker of a smile, and answered him in the language of Judah.

"The King of Kings is angry with your king. He sent to him to come before him at Lachish, for judgment, and he did not come."

"Nor will he," said Eliakim, still in the language spoken by the Assyrians.

The Rab Shaka was not smiling now.

"Who has given him this counsel?"

Eliakim was silent.

"Have *you* given him this counsel?"

The Rab Shaka had leaned forward, his eyes hard as black iron. For the first time, the lord Eliakim quailed. The Rab Shaka was a man who could inspire fear.

"No," said the Assyrian scornfully. "Not you. And my king says this: 'In whom do you trust, that you rebel against me?'"

He turned suddenly to the Tartan, who took hold of the Kushite boy and thrust him before the three men of Judah.

"You trust in the staff of this bruised reed!" shouted the Rab Shaka. "In Egypt on which, if a man lean, it will go into his hand and pierce it! So is Pharaoh, king of Egypt, to all that trust in him! See how he stands before you!"

And Taharka stood before them—before the three

men, before the people on the wall, for the wall was now crowded with the people of the city. He stood there, a king—"Pharaoh, king of Egypt." This was the use the Assyrians had had for him in Jerusalem. This was the return they had had in mind.

He had never before felt such shame.

The people were very still. Pharaoh, king of Egypt, in whom they had indeed placed their trust, a prisoner in the hands of the Assyrians?

I'll speak to them, thought Taharka. I'll cry out to them that I am not Pharaoh, king of Egypt, that it's a lie.

But he did not have a chance to speak.

The Rab Shaka sprang to his feet. He held out his arms to the people on the wall. His voice outrang the voice of the crier.

"Hear the words of my king! Do not let Hezekiah deceive you, for he will not be able to deliver you out of my hand!"

His voice became the voice of a father, exhorting his prodigal children to come home.

"Do not listen to Hezekiah. Listen to my king. He says to you, 'Make an agreement with me. Come to me. You are hungry, you are thirsty. Come out to me and every man will eat of his own vine and his own fig tree, and every one will drink the waters of his well.'

"Have no fear of my king. He comes to take you away to a land like your own land, a land of corn and wine, a land of olive oil and honey, a land of bread and vineyards, that you may live and not die!"

His voice dripped scorn.

"And do not listen to your king when he tells you your God will deliver you. What god among all the nations has delivered his country out of our hands, that your God should deliver Jerusalem?"

The people on the wall were silent, strangely silent. What were they thinking? thought Taharka. Far off as they were, hidden by the turrets, he could not see them clearly; but he thought they must be very thin, hollow-eyed, like the elderly lord of the household and the two scribes. Their food must be very low. They must be hungry. What would they do in order, as the Rab Shaka had said, to live and not die?

The Rab Shaka, too, was wondering. His gaze swept the wall, searching the faces. He listened, waiting for the first cry of surrender, the first outburst of rebellion against the Judahite king.

But still there was no sound.

The Assyrian returned to his chair. He beckoned the lord Eliakim close. He leaned forward and, for a long time, stared at the old man with a look of malevolence Taharka had never seen before, chilling the boy's heart like a cold mist. What was in the Assyrian's mind? If his words of "mercy" had not prevailed, what next? Some terrible act of warning? Taharka thought of the scenes at Lachish and shuddered.

The old man stood tall. His eyes did not waver. After a while, the Rab Shaka leaned back in his chair. His eyes were like the eyes of a lion robbed of its prey but his voice was calm, almost careless.

"You have heard the words of my king. Return with them, to yours."

He waved him away, as if dismissing a troublesome servant. The lord Eliakim bowed, still the simple bow of courtesy and, straight and firm as ever, returned to the gate of the city.

There was a long silence. The Assyrian turned to Taharka.

"You have heard, Kushite. My words were for you, too. But what you have been offered today, whoever you may be, is far beyond the dreams of those people on the wall of this little city, or of that old servant of a little rebel king." He nodded to Taharka's guard. "Take him back to his tent."

Taharka sat alone in his tent. The night outside was dark, moonless. The voice hummed in his ears, sweet and purring, ringing and wild.

"Come to me! Make an agreement with me!— What would the king of kings ask in return? So little, really—"

So little really. For what? The double crown. The downfall of Shabataka. Shepnuset—

And for those who said no—

"Haru. Hawk. Great One."

The voice, soft and hissing, came from the foot of the flap of the tent. Someone had passed Taharka's guard, snaking low on the ground through the dark of the night. Someone slithered beneath the flap, then rose to his feet, shaking dust and earth from his garments.

It was Amos.

❧ 21 ❧

The Spring and the Tunnel

"I SAID I would see you at Jerusalem."

"But how—?"

"Keep your voice down! This guard can't hear, but others may."

"He's asleep?" Taharka was astounded. Assyrian guards did not sleep.

"A sleep deep as Sheol," said Amos grimly. He looked a little puzzled. "There was something strange about that. It seemed to me that he fell before I struck him."

But for the moment Taharka could think only of the amazing fact that Amos was here, his friend.

"I'm glad you're here, no matter how," he said. And he added in a kind of wonder. "I have been so alone."

Amos glanced around the tent, the cushions, the sheep skins, the lingering odor of the food that had been brought for Taharka's evening meal.

"This doesn't look like a prison."

"It's a prison," said Taharka bitterly. "Amos, what

have you done? You were out of the trap. Now you have walked back into it."

"Crawled back in," Amos corrected him, brushing off a bur. "And I have not come to walk into a trap. I have come to get you out of one. And into another." He put his hands on the boy's shoulders, shaking him a little. "Are you listening, Haru? I have come to take you into Jerusalem. I have come to take you to my king."

The tent was very quiet. Taharka did not move. Amos stepped back, as if chilled. He looked again around the tent, then back at Taharka, his eyes now puzzled and uncertain.

"Are you listening?" he said again.

Taharka spoke at last.

"I was thinking of Hermes," he said.

It was as if someone else had spoken. He was as surprised as Amos to hear the words. But in his mind was the echo of other words—his own words, spoken to Sabi, the Mucri boy.

"Hermes is a Nile donkey, a royal donkey. He must not serve the Assyrians."

He must not serve the Assyrians.

"Yes," he said. "I am listening. What do we have to do?"

Even as he spoke, Amos watched him closely with that considering, uncertain look.

"There are no stars," he said, "and not far from the outer wall of the city, if we can reach it, is a spring of water. From there—" He stopped. "What

have the Assyrians offered you, Great One? Your
life?"

That and more, thought Taharka, but he answered
only, "For a price. I don't want to pay that price."

"I can promise you nothing," said Amos. "In spite
of all, I believe that Jerusalem will be delivered. Remember the omen of the sun? But I cannot ask you
to believe it. And beyond that . . ."

"It doesn't matter," said Taharka, "if I believe it or
not. I will not serve the Assyrians."

Amos let out his breath in a long sigh.

"Good," he said. "Then get rid of that rich robe,
young Hawk. It will hamper your wings."

To the east of the city not far, as Amos had said,
from the great wall, was a spring of water, the pool
of Gihon. Here the people of Jerusalem had always
come out to descend the steps cut into the rock and
gather their precious supplies of water.

Sealed inside their walls by the Assyrian patrols,
they could not come out now. Jerusalem's water supply had been cut off. It must be very low, the Assyrians had thought, if not exhausted. And, since in the
short run, water was even more necessary than food,
they had begun to wonder.

Two soldiers guarded the spring, just in case. Amos
and Taharka, inching their way over the rough ground,
shielded by the dark of the night, watched the two

men in the light from their fire, passing and re-pass-ing.

Taharka was armed with a sword. He had taken it from the guard, who lay where he had fallen, outside the tent.

And now Taharka knew, watching the distant gleam of the two men's armor, that this time there would be need for killing. He stomach tightened. He had been trained for battle. Once long ago, to save a life, he had killed a beast. But a man?

And why? Why had Amos brought him here? This was no road to the city.

Amos said only, "You will see. You will see the wisdom of my king."

Now he whispered, "After this, no talk. So listen carefully. We slide the rest of the way. Slide, not crawl, like snakes. Until we come to the light from their fire. Then, when I give the signal, we are up and upon them. I take the big one. You take the other."

Taharka had not been taught to slide or crawl upon the ground. Such training had not been thought necessary for a god. Amos, on the other hand, had been trained in the old ways of his people, the ways of the desert. He did indeed move with the ease and swiftness of a snake. For a moment, Taharka thought he could not keep up with him. His heart bursting, he struggled in the wake of his friend, hardly notic-ing the scrapes on elbows and arms and knees, in his desire to do his part.

They had reached the edge of the circle of light.
For a moment they lay prone, regaining their strength.
The bigger, older sentry said something to the younger
one, who did not reply. Taharka thought that the
man's steps were somehow uneven, not the steady,
dogged tramp of the older man. But he had no time
to think about it. Amos's hand was on his arm, his
voice hissing in his ear.

"Now!"

They were up and into the light from the fire.
Suddenly Taharka was very calm. There was a job to
be done. He knew how to do it, and he was doing
it.

The guards were trained for surprise, and their
swords were in their hands. Still, the sudden attack
was a shock and they were at the first disadvantage.
Taharka's man sprang back, staggering a little, and
for a moment the boy thought he had him right at
the start. But the man was a skilled swordsman and
Taharka's blow was parried, jarring the youth back.
The guard followed up on his advantage, and Taharka's foot struck a rock. He was falling. He rolled
on the ground, just beyond the deadly, downward
thrust that would have pinned him to the earth. Embutah's voice rang in his ears: "Too slow, little nephew!
Move your sacred back!" And he was on his feet
again, running right at his adversary.

But the guard was quick. His sword was free and
in play again. Iron clashed on iron, clashed and slid;

and the tall, slight youth and the shorter, burlier man were locked in a test of strength that must surely go against Taharka.

There was a cry of agony. Amos had made his kill. And then—so suddenly that the Kushite youth was thrown off balance—Taharka's man reeled back. As the boy watched, unbelieving, the sword wavered in the young guard's hand, then fell. His face was a strange, grayish color. And, though Taharka's sword had not grazed him, he collapsed upon the ground.

Taharka approached him, his sword half at the ready. He felt Amos' hand on his shoulder.

"Let him be. There is no need."

Completely confused, Taharka stammered, "He's sick. Something's wrong with him. I should—"

"In the name of the Almighty One! You're not a physician now. You're an escaped prisoner and this man would be your pursuer. Come! There is not time!"

Half dragged, stumbling and bewildered, Taharka was forced away by his friend. The torches of the guards had fallen on the ground and, at first, the boy could not see where they were going. Then Amos took one of them up and raised it high and he saw that they were approaching the spring.

"What are you doing? Where are you taking me?"

"Quiet. Trust me. We are going into the city."

A flight of steps, cut into the rock, led down into the well. Amos stepped down onto the topmost step.

"Follow," he said. "Be quick."

Down they crept till the cold, clear water of the spring lapped their feet.

"Can you swim?" said Amos.

"Of course." Embutah had taught him that, too, along the green banks of the river so far, far away. "But why? Jerusalem does not lie at the bottom of a pool!"

"Follow me," said Amos. "But not too close. I must keep the torch burning."

Into the water, so cold at first, then almost warm against the chill of the night air. Amos trod the water, holding the torch high above his head, casting light and shadows against the wall of rock. And then they saw it, half submerged, half open, a great gaping hole in the rock.

"It's here!" hissed Amos. There was a note of relief in his voice.

"What is?"

"When my king destroyed the altar to the god of Nineveh," whispered Amos, "he knew there was the chance that Jerusalem would come under siege. That was when he built the outer wall to the south. And inside that wall—Here. Hold the torch."

Taharka took the brand, treading swiftly, fearful of dousing the precious light. Amos clambered onto the edge of the hole, retrieved the torch, and moved back.

"Come," he said, and there was a strange, hollow, echoing sound to his voice.

Taharka followed him, his feet slipping against the wet stones. Once he was sure of his footing, he tried to stand straight, but found he could not. But he could stand half stooping, peering ahead into what the light from the torch revealed.

It was a long, low passageway, leading ever downward, through which the water from the spring gurgled and rushed, rising as high as their hips.

"Come," said Amos again and, holding the torch ahead of him, led the way into the passage.

"Inside that wall," he said, as if he had not been distracted, "he dug a hole, lined with rock. The 'pool' of Siloam, we have called it. It was no pool when I left my country for yours, just a dry ditch; but already the tunnelers had begun boring through the rock, under the wall. The tunnel was to end here, at the spring of Gihon, and the pool of Siloam was to be fed from here. When I heard how long the city has been cut off from the water of Gihon, I knew it must have been completed. The Assyrians have barred the people from food, but not from their water."

Ever downward led the tunnel. Taharka's neck and back ached, the cold wet tunic clung to his body, the precious water swirled and rushed about his legs. Yes, this Hezekiah was a wise king, a king with foresight. He had kept his people alive. For what? To die on the stakes or in the slave coffles of the Assyrians? The tunnel led on into the darkness. To what else did it lead but the darkness of death?

Not far down the way, the passage curved, still cutting into the rock.

"Why has he done this?" said Taharka, and the walls seemed to echo: Why has he done this? "Why did they not cut straight through?"

"The tomb of David lies in this rock," said Amos. "My king would not disturb his grave."

David, the warrior king. A king who had made his people one and strong. A king remembered for 300 years. Who would remember Taharka? Indeed, after tomorrow, who would remember David?

They had come to the end of the waterway.

"This is it," said Amos. "The pool of Siloam. And see? No longer a bed of dried mud. See? Flowing with the life-giving waters from Gihon! How they must have wondered, the Assyrians! We must swim again, Hawk. Douse the torch, we have no more need of it. We're here!"

A low rock wall rose above the pool. They swam to the steps and climbed to the top. For a moment the joy of Amos' homecoming infected even Taharka.

Then he looked around him.

A little warren of streets, like any other town, leading to a main entrance and a wider street that disappeared into the darkness. Where were the torches? Where were the people milling about the arcades, savoring the night air?

Silence. He had never known a city so silent.

"They will stay tonight behind the walls of their

houses," said Amos. "They will cling to their families. They will pray. Before dawn, they will come out. They will come again to the wall. But this time they will come with their weapons in their hands."

Something was stirring, not far away. A child was crying, a fretful, whining wail. A woman, little more than a girl, was feebly trying to fill a water jug. The child clung to her robe. A woman of Jerusalem, one of the people he had seen that day on the wall. This time he could see clearly.

Horror turned him cold. He had seen terrible sights, but not like this. It was as if two skeletons from his old anatomy class had come to life, just barely, and were trying to drink.

He started to his feet. Amos laid a hand on his shoulder.

"They are dying of hunger. Can you cure that, doctor?"

"I can help her fill her jug!"

But the woman had managed it herself. She and the child slipped away into the shadows.

"Come," said Amos. "I will take you to my king."

≫ 22 ≪

The Mad King

THE HILL rose high above the city. On it stood the high house of the king and the temple of their God, where all could see. Taharka remembered from the stories in Napata that a king named Solomon had built them, and encased them with gold. They weren't very big. Mostly of brick, shored up with wood like the houses of ordinary people along the Nile. The temple, especially, had a shabby look, a look of disrepair. As for the gold, it had been there, and some of it was left, but most had been stripped away. Tribute to the Assyrians or some other king, he supposed.

Soldiers of Judah patrolled outside the house of the king. Not very many and they were far from the smart guards of the temple complex in Thebes. There were torches here, and Amos stepped into the light.

He was a well known figure in the city. Many hopes had been pinned on him. Taharka, hooded and hidden in the shadows, heard the whispers, rising into a babble of voices.

"Amos ben Neriah!"

"The ambassador!"

"He's back! How can it be? How did he get in?"

"Is there news? Is there hope? The Egyptians, the Kushites! Is there any hope?"

Then all discipline collapsed. They pressed in on him, hands reaching out to touch him, eyes searching his face, hungry for hope, one last hope for life. Taharka saw the pain in Amos' face. He was back, but his hands were empty. He had brought them nothing, thought Taharka bitterly, but Taharka himself. A refugee, a helpless exile, the Assyrians' pet "Pharaoh."

A figure had appeared in one of the high windows that rose above the porch.

"Soldiers of Judah!"

It was the old man Eliakim, the head of the king's household. The thin, worn old man who, with trembling courage, had faced the Rab Shaka and refused the lion his prey.

"Back to your posts! Captain! Control your men!"

Amos drew closer and raised his hand in greeting. As in the long ago audience room in Thebes, Taharka could see that he was close to exhaustion.

"Eliakim."

"Amos. Amos ben Neriah."

The old man had raised his hands in wonder. His voice shook.

"Let them pass. Come in, Amos. Come in to the house of the king."

It was big enough after all. The high, heavy wooden pillars cast long shadows that shielded Taharka from the eyes of the soldiers. But when they had passed the men and mounted to the long porch, when old Eliakim came hurrying down along the cedar columns to meet them, Taharka let the cloth fall away from his face.

At first, Eliakim did not notice. In trembling haste he approached the ambassador, with trembling arms he embraced him.

"Amos ben Neriah. I give thanks for your safety."

He drew back, holding the ambassador at arms' length. Like the soldiers, he gazed upon the face of Amos. Like the eyes of the soldiers, his eyes begged for hope. Is there any hope? Do you bring us any hope?

Then, in the light of the torches, he saw the face of Taharka. He remembered, from outside the wall. The Kushite boy. Pharaoh, the captive king of Egypt. How or why he did not know or, at that moment, care. He only knew that this was all Amos had brought him. He only knew that there was no more hope.

He straightened. Dignified and respectful, the head of the king's household.

"I will take you to Hezekiah the King."

They waited in a reception room in the royal apartments, outside a little office. The king was working late that night, but that was the only sign of anything unusual. Eliakim had gone in before them to inform the king, and there was a hum of voices through the open door. Taharka had a strange feeling. It was somehow like the time he had waited with Talos outside the little surgery in Thebes, to be interviewed by Baku.

Eliakim came out of the office.

"He will receive you now. He is very busy, you know. He is working on the plans to improve the grain depots."

Busy? Plans to improve the grain depots in a city about to be destroyed? Taharka felt a little dizzy. A madman. He was about to be presented to a madman. With real apprehension, he followed Amos into the office.

A secretary was rolling up his papyrus, gathering up his writing tools. He looked unhappy. The other man, resting on cushions, was talking softly, urgently.

"And you make it plain to Nahum. The sheds face south. *South.*"

"Yes, lord, but he isn't going to like it."

"He doesn't have to like it! Who is king here, and who's the carpenter? If—"

The shadows fell across the light. The man on the cushions raised his eyes. Then, slowly, he rose to his feet.

The mad king. *He* was not very big either. Not very young, but his eyes were the eyes of a young man. He wore a robe of some kind of coarse cloth, but the bands on his arms were of gold.

He turned to the secretary and, for a moment, his eyes were only for the younger man. He laid his hands on his shoulders.

"You can go, Chilon," he said. "It's enough now. You get some sleep."

Nothing else was said but, in those few words, the game they had been playing was over. They were two friends saying goodbye, probably forever. There were tears in the eyes of the young scribe as he bowed himself from the room.

The king watched him go. Somber-eyed, he drew shut the door. Then he turned back and spread his arms wide.

"Amos ben Neriah."

The two men embraced like brothers.

"So you made it back, Amos. I expected you would. I can guess how." His eyes sparkled like the eyes of a boy looking for praise. "How did you like my tunnel?"

"It was wet, my lord!" And they laughed together like conspirators.

"Yes," said Hezekiah, "I thought it was a good idea. All these weeks, the Assyrians must have been very puzzled. So you're back. And you have brought me—'Pharaoh, king of Egypt.' "

Taharka stood straight and still as the little king of Judah looked him over with his bright, curious eyes. Hezekiah glanced at Amos.

"The real thing?" he said.

"The real thing."

And Hezekiah became the courteous monarch, greeting a fellow ruler.

"Pharaoh. Welcome." He gestured downward to his rough robe. "Forgive the sackcloth." He made a wry face. "Goatskin. Not the most comfortable. But I have been to the temple to pray, and there was no time to change. And, after all, I come from a family of shepherds."

Taharka found himself laughing.

"My grandfather was a boat-builder!"

"I would offer you food, but it seems the last of it is gone." Hezekiah spoke as if this were some minor annoyance. He gestured them to the cushions and drew up a chair for himself. "So," he said, "welcome to our city. You have courage to come here." He added dryly, "Some would call it something else."

Two mad kings, thought Taharka. But he said only, "I had no place else to go."

"I'm sure there were other choices. We saw one of them yesterday, at the wall. How did you get away from them?"

He listened with interest as Taharka and Amos recounted the escape. When they told of the death of the guard, the strange collapse of the sentry at the spring, his face sobered, his eyes became intense.

"Strange," he said softly, "strange. Like an omen."

Like a prophecy." There was a pause, and then he
asked. "But how did Pharaoh come to be here, and
not with his army? How were you captured?"

Briefly Amos sketched the story of the last few
weeks: The death of the taster. The escape from the
great house in Thebes. Shabataka's treachery. The
crossing of the desert.

At the end Hezekiah commented, "So they let
you down through a window! Like our king David.
It seems it's as well for kings to have strong legs."

His interest prompted Taharka to speak. He was
telling Hezekiah more and more, things he had almost forgotten. Hezekiah was fascinated by the story
of Baku and his patients, of Taharka's trials as a
physician's apprentice.

"I would have liked that! What an opportunity for
a young man born as you were born. Do you realize
your good fortune?"

And at the story of the healing of Sabi: "Why
that's what they did for me when I was so ill from a
boil! Is it really a remedy for a horse?" He shouted
with laughter.

Then he turned sober.

"That illness. That healing. There was something
strange about that." His gaze again became intense.
"Something wonderful."

For some reason, Taharka felt a tingling along his
spine.

"Jahveh our God had told the prophet, the man
called Isaiah, that I would die of this illness. But the

people had great need of me, and I prayed to Jahveh to be merciful to them and to me. And you see I am still alive. He sent me a sign. A great one."

"Yes," whispered Taharka. "I remember! The earth trembled and the shadow on the sundial moved back. The sun moved back."

"So you saw it!"

A God of mercy, thought Taharka. A God who could heal a king by moving back time. But had Hezekiah been saved from illness only to die by the hand of the Assyrians?

They fell silent. Hezekiah said at last:

"What a life you have had. What choices you have been offered! What choices may still lie ahead." He looked at him as if searching for something behind his eyes.

"What is it you want?"

What did he want? He wanted to live, that was what he wanted. And it seemed that that was what he could not have. The sky, through the windows, was not so dark now. Dawn would come soon. The last dawn he would ever see. Still—Hezekiah's eyes compelled him to think.

"I don't know," he said at last. "To live as a man, maybe. Just a man." To walk among people, he thought. To laugh with my friends, to find work again, to help and heal—

That, or the double crown of the Two Lands. The docks at Napata, the black mud of the Nile. Shepnuset. All these came with the double crown.

But it was given to me by chance, he thought, and taken away again. I cannot have it back. Unless, and he thought of the words of the Rab Shaka, I serve the Assyrians.

The sky outside the windows was turning red and gold. Suddenly he was angry. What were they talking about anyway? Was this man really mad, really a fool after all? He looked into Hezekiah's eyes and said what none of them had spoken of before.

"I don't really have to make choices, do I? After tomorrow—after today—it won't really matter."

"I don't know," Hezekiah said in his turn. "Our God has promised Isaiah we will be delivered from the Assyrian. 'He will return the way he came,' he said. 'He will not come into the city.' " Then the king of Judah smiled. "That choice is Jahveh's, to save or to destroy. But as for me, one way or another, I will not serve the Assyrians."

"Nor will I!" And Taharka knew he meant it, even if somehow he survived what was to come.

"My lord. My lord the king."

It was the old man Eliakim. And the sky, now, was pale.

"My lord, you must come."

The king of Judah rose slowly from his chair. No more talk. No more plans for the future. The time had come.

Taharka, too, had risen. And now, in his mind, there was room for only one thought.

This is the day of my death.

Neither of them noticed the face of Eliakim. It was not the face of a man contemplating the end. There was a puzzled look in his eyes, a look almost of excitement.

He had come from the wall. And he had seen something strange.

≥ 23 ≤

"He Will not Come into the City"

THE WALL was dark with the defenders of the city. Their weapons were indeed in their hands—their swords, their spears and arrows, their oil-soaked torches, fires burning at the ready. So had it been with the defenders of Lachish. What good had it done *them*?

Taharka stood with Hezekiah, Amos at his side, the king's honor guard close by. He had come out to stand against them. If he must die, he would die like the people of the city. The streets were not empty now. They surged below the wall—men, women, children—clubs, rocks, knives, home-made slings. They pressed toward the west gate as if they were the attackers, eager for the assault. But Taharka, from the wall, could see the real assailants, across the open space—the black tents, the siege engines and chariots, the battering rams, the horses. Once he had stood among them and watched their work of terror. Now he faced them. Now he was their prey. Soon they would close in. Soon they would blot out the rising sun.

He had been given sword and spear. He remembered Embutah. "This is a spear, little nephew. You grasp it so—" The *ka* of Embutah would stand beside him. He would give it no cause for shame.

Why did they not move? The sky was red now. It was time. They were ready for attack, the chariots positioned, the rams in place, the horses drawn up. Surely they were ready.

Something was wrong.

"Where is their infantry?" whispered Amos.

Yes, where were the men? The horses were there. Where were the riders? The siege engines were there. Where were the men who would sweat and strain to drive them forward? And the silence. Where were the shouts of the commanders? Hezekiah, the sweat on *his* brow, muttered to himself.

"What is this? Some trickery?"

But there was movement among those black tents. Carts and wagons were being drawn up.

"Loading," said Amos. "*What* are they loading?"

Something strange was happening. What use did they have for those carts? The cold fear of the unknown took hold of the men on the wall, spread in waves to the people below.

What strange and terrible thing did they have in store for them?

The silence was broken. Someone was shouting out there in the open space between the city and the camp, a wild piercing cry. A young boy, a shepherd, was running across the fields, one lone young boy. They could not make out the words.

"A trick, a trick!" hissed Amos. And "A trick! A trick!" ran from mouth to mouth among the soldiers. One of them had strung his bow, notched his arrow.

"Hold!" shouted the king. And "Hold your weapons!" ran along line among the captains. And now they could understand the words.

"It's over! Open the gate! Let me in!"

"Throw him a rope," said the burly captain of Hezekiah's guard.

Jerusalem might fall to the battering rams, not some Assyrian deviltry. Let them work for their victory.

A line was dropped and the boy, strong and lithe from his work in the pastures, clambered the height of the wall. He was surrounded by the soldiers, shoved roughly from one to the other.

"An Assyrian spy!"

"What's his story?"

"It had better be good!"

"Take him to the king."

They threw him, trembling and terrified, at the feet of Hezekiah. He looked up, forgetting his fear for a moment, in amazement and awe.

"You're the king?"

"Get up, boy," said Hezekiah. "Say what you came to say."

Still trembling, a little unsteady, the boy stood up.

"It's over," he mumbled, the words muffled by the clamor rising around them.

"Speak up!"

This time it was almost a scream.

"It's over!"

Suddenly everything was still.

"What are you saying?" said Hezekiah. "Who are you?"

"They drafted me into their camp," said the boy. "To clean up after them. I saw what's happening. There's sickness there. They're all sick. They're dying. They're dropping like flies. They're moving out."

"It could be true," broke in Taharka. "I saw it myself. Last night."

They looked from one to another. They couldn't take it in. But Taharka gazed out across the field; and then, in that stunned silence, he heard it, thin and faint, carried by the wind, the keening and the cries of the stricken Assyrians. And, in the distance, he could see what was being loaded onto those carts. The bodies of men. The sick, the dying and the dead.

For just a moment, he was stricken with horror. He should go to them. He should be there. It was his calling to help them. Surely a real physician could do something against that terrible wave of death.

But Amos was looking at him with a look that reminded him, just a little, of Shabataka.

"Don't be a fool," he muttered.

And Hezekiah had closed his eyes. "He will not come into the city," he whispered. Then he opened them wide. The words came in a great shout. "He will not come into the city!"

The word had spread among the people, from mouth to mouth, and the voices rose around them.

"It's over!"

"A plague has struck them down!"

"It's over! Praise to Jahveh!"

"They're moving out!"

"We're going to live!"

"He will not come into the city!"

A captain of a hundred pushed his way through to the king.

"My lord the king, there's trouble at the west gate."

Hezekiah knew without words. The people of Jerusalem had suffered greatly. There were few who had not lost friends or family to the Assyrian drive and, before that, to their demands for human tribute. They had been trapped and starved, shut in from their fields and vineyards, "like birds in a cage." They wanted revenge. They were burning for revenge, as if swept by a great fire.

"Hold them back," said Hezekiah.

"I don't know if we can. They're trying to break through. They're tearing out door posts for rams."

"I'll go to them," said Hezekiah. "They won't turn against me now. This is the Lord's work, not ours."

And, gathering his cloak around him, he laughed softly.

It was over. They had loaded their dead and their dying onto their carts and wagons and moved out. They were gone. The echoes of the moans and the cries were still.

Once, across the fields, Taharka had seen a lone figure lifted onto a rich litter and carried away. He had recognized the brightness of the robe. The Rab Shaka. He had seen it raise a fist toward the city.

"We will be back," it seemed to say.

But Taharka's death day had come and gone, and he was still alive. The people of the city were still alive.

They had held back from pursuit. Hezekiah had been right. If they would not turn against him in surrender, they would not turn against him in this. "Jackals' work," said Amos contemptuously.

But later, when the sun was high, the gates had finally been thrown open and they had poured out— out into the fields of barley, to the spring of Gihon, to the orchards and the vineyards. Cartloads of grain to the grinding stones, cartloads and armloads of vegetables and fruits to the city.

They were going to live!

Figs and dates and honey cakes, platters of leeks and root vegetables were brought to the table of the king that evening, for the first time in many weeks. The shepherd boy had provided a ram from his father's herds. Taharka found that he could eat very little. He, after all, had not been suffering from hunger. But he had not slept for two days and a night. He wanted only to sleep. And later, as the sun went down, he wandered outside his chamber, to the roof of the house of the king.

Down there, in the streets, he could hear the voices. Not far off, there was music. People were dancing. If he could have moved that far, he would have gone down and joined them. The last thing he thought before he fell asleep was:

I'm going to live!

Sleep wrapped him like a dark cloak.

And then, suddenly he was wide awake.

It was not morning. The moon was high in the sky. Something had startled him out of that darkness, his eyes wide, his muscles tense, his hand already feeling for the short sword that still hung at his side.

Someone was on the roof. A man. He was leaning over, coiling the rope he must have used to scale the wall of the king's house. An assassin, thought Taharka, not quite believing it. From where? Sent by whom? And who was his target?

Silent as a cat, Taharka inched his way into the darkness behind a corner of the wall. The sword was in his hand now.

The man straightened, the rope slung over his

shoulder. He shook his head as if confused and looked around him, unsure of what to do next. Then, hesitating a little, he made his way toward the entrance that led to Taharka's chamber.

Taharka was behind him. The point of his sword was at his back.

"Don't move," he said.

The man froze still as death. For some reason, Taharka did not call out for a guard.

"Now," he said, "Turn around. Slowly."

Very slowly, the man obeyed. And then, to Taharka's amazement, he shielded his eyes with his hands and fell to his knees.

But not before Taharka had seen his face.

He was not a man of the city. He was a black man, a man from the Egyptian southland. There was a scar, not very old, just over his left eye.

☙ 24 ☙

The Man With the Scar

"GET UP," said Taharka. The man rose to his feet, but still shielded his eyes.

"Take your hands away from your face," said Taharka. "Who do you think I am?"

"I know who you are, Great God," said the man, "Amon forgive me, I have seen your face. Many times. It was necessary."

"Then," said Taharka impatiently, "if you are still able to see me, what are you afraid of? Let me look at you."

The man removed his hands and raised his head. In the light from the moon, Taharka could see the scar, just above the left eye. It was the same man. The man in the street. The man on the delta border who had raised his hand in farewell.

"So," said Taharka, "you have seen my face many times. It was necessary. Of course. An assassin must be sure he has the right man." The point of the sword was still at the man's chest.

186

"I'm not an assassin," the man protested. "I'm a—" he stopped.

"A what?" said Taharka, glancing at the coiled rope. "A cat burglar?"

A cat burglar! Shepnuset, far away on the roof of that other Great House in Thebes. "He says he was a cat burglar."

"Who are you? What's your name?"

"I am Kefmose," said the man, adding proudly, "Kefmose the Cat. I guard the Holy of Holies in the temple at Thebes. That is," he added, "I did."

"Come," said Taharka. He prodded the man toward the entry way and, following, sheathed his sword. "Sit," he said, as they entered the chamber. The lamp was burning. He had brought some dates from the table of the king. "Eat, if you're hungry," he said.

He was. And, as he helped himself to the fruit, Taharka settled himself on the cushions.

"Why?" he said. "You've been following me all along. In Thebes, to the delta, across the desert— how did you manage *that*? Why?"

"She told me to," said the man called Kefmose, through a mouthful of dates.

"She?"

"The Lady. The Priestess."

Shepnuset. Taharka felt as if someone had struck him a blow in the chest, as if Shepnuset herself had appeared in the little chamber.

"What she tells me to do, I do," said Kefmose.

"She saved my life once, when they would have had me beaten and I fought back. She got me the job in the Temple. She said she might have use for me later, and she did."

And as Taharka listened, humbled and shamed by his old doubts of the girl who loved him, Kefmose told him the story.

He had indeed been a cat burglar as a boy—the highest rank in the profession!—working for a gang boss, the master of a band of child thieves. But he had gotten away from the man, tried to find honest work and had a hard time of it, and finally joined the army. One of his duties had been to arrest his old master. Out of revenge, the man had betrayed his past.

"And," said Kefmose indignantly, "he even lied about my rank—said I was a purse snatcher!"

Sentenced to be beaten for fraud, he had defended himself and been cut down by a sword blow to the head—"That's how I got the scar"—and taken before the High Priest, who had sentenced him to death.

"But the Lady said no, and when the Lady says no, it's no. She said she liked people with spirit, and there were things I could do for her. There were, sooner than we expected. I'm the one who got her into the Holy of Holies and barricaded it when the pretender came, just before the wedding. *He* wasn't the bridegroom!"

So she had really done it! And it's true, thought Taharka. With all his power and determination, Shabataka had not won against her. She loves *me!*

"When you left the Great House," said Kefmose, "she told me to follow you. Wherever you went. If you got into trouble, I was to get you out of it. 'You'll know what to do,' she said. But it seems, Great God, that you're not so bad after all at taking care of yourself."

With a little help from my friends and perhaps a god or two, thought Taharka.

"I suppose," said Kefmose, "that at the time she didn't know what following you was going to mean. But she told me to do it, and I did it."

Taharka looked at him in wonder.

"*How* did you do it? The desert. How did you get across the desert?"

"That was the easy part. The army again. I joined up with him."

He rose suddenly, suddenly frowning.

"That's why I'm here."

"Yes, why are you here? After all these weeks, why do you suddenly show yourself? I'm safe now, no need to watch over me any more. Now you can go back, tell Shepnuset—"

He stopped. What message did he have for Shepnuset? That they would never see each other again?

"Should I tell her you're coming back?" asked Kefmose. "With the army?"

Taharka stared at him helplessly.

"These new friends of yours, here in Jerusalem. Could they help?"

"How could they help?"

"Yes, that's what I thought," said Kefmose gloomily. "But there is something you ought to know, you and your friends. It's why I came here tonight."

Taharka waited as the man finished the last date.

"One thing about my old gang boss," said Kefmose. "He taught me a lot. He taught me how to listen for things people didn't want known. I'm a good spy. That's how I found you. I heard from the Mucri that you had been captured and I have been tracking you down ever since. But while I was with the pretender, I thought I might as well keep an ear open. It's a good thing I did."

"Go on," said Taharka.

"This king of Judah," said Kefmose. "He thinks he's safe now. But he's not."

"What do you mean?" But already Taharka had begun to understand.

"The pretender knows he's going to have trouble at home. He's had news. The Priestess. A lot of people are loyal to her. They will have heard of the Assyrians' victory. And if he goes back defeated, his tail between his legs—"

"But," said Taharka slowly, "if he goes back the conqueror of Judah, the conqueror of Canaan like Rameses the Great—"

"That's the plan. Cartloads of tribute. Slaves. Maybe even the king of Judah in a cage."

Taharka felt a little sick.

Sennacherib. Shabataka. Where was the difference? Evil was evil, wherever it arose.

Choices, Hezekiah had said. The time had come when the choice must be made, for good and all.

He thought of Hezekiah, asleep in the king's chamber, dreaming of the prospect of life.

He thought of Shepnuset, brave little Shepnuset and the asp, the girl who loved him and had watched over him from afar, the brave Lady gathering her supporters to stand against the usurper.

But how long could she do it alone?

A grim smile played around Taharka's lips. His life had been given back to him by some twist of fate or hand of a god. Now, once again, it hung in the balance. But he had made his choice. He would do his part and let the gods decide!

"So," said Hezekiah, "You will go to the army. We of Judah thank you. But will it work?"

Taharka had gone with Kefmose and Amos to bring the warning to the king. Already there had been news. The Kushite army had not returned to the Nile. It was camped not far away.

"They would want him back," said Kefmose. "Except for his Somali guards, the army does not favor this king. The portents have not been good. The sun has done strange things, the earth has trembled, the army has been defeated. Not all of them really believe he's the god."

"But what will they think *me?*" said Taharka. "A pretender. None of them know my face."

"I can vouch for you, Great God," said Kefmose.

"Who would believe you?" said Taharka bluntly. "Besides, I will not put you in this peril. Whatever happens, the Priestess will need you in Thebes."

Hezekiah had risen to his feet.

"You do not have to do this. We took our chances with Sennacherib. We will take our chances with this Shabataka."

"No," said Taharka. "I will play out this game to the end. Two impossible things have happened already and perhaps one more will happen now."

"I will send you out with the army," said Hezekiah. "I will ride at your side. The king of Judah and his army, restoring Pharaoh to his men—"

"They'll cut you down. You will only hasten the ruin of your people. The Kushites couldn't stand against the Assyrians but, forgive me, no army of Judah can stand against *them*." And he said what, in his heart, he had always felt was true: "I must face him alone."

Amos spoke for the first time.

"Not alone."

He too rose to his feet. He began to pace restlessly about the room.

"Listen," he said. "This could succeed." And to Kefmose, "You say the army is not completely loyal to this Pharaoh?"

"I've been one of them," said Kefmose. "I've heard what they say when the captains aren't listening. They remember who the golden wand pointed to. Some think this man has murdered the true god, and that he's under a curse."

"So, if they had a choice—"

Kefmose snorted. "When did they ever have a choice?"

"Let's give them a choice," said Amos. He smiled at Taharka. "Remember Talos and the stories of his people? Let's let them choose their king."

"How will we do that?"

"First," said Amos, "you must *not* face him alone. That is the one thing you must not do. The people must be there to witness. No message, no warning, no private meeting surrounded by his guards. We will ride out, you and I, to their camp. I will be your spokesman, your 'Rab Shaka,' but they won't know that. You will not ride out as a king, no royal robe, nothing to draw attention at first. A herald will announce us—an ambassador from the king of Judah, with a message for Pharaoh king of Egypt. Now, what do you suppose they will think this message is?"

"An offer," said Hezekiah. "An offer of tribute. A bribe to make them turn around and go home."

"Exactly," said Amos. "Never fear, they'll let us in."

"And then—" Amos stopped. He didn't know. "And then," he said at last, "what will happen, will happen."

"You know," said Taharka, "that you're going to your death."

"What choice do I have? What choice do any of us have?" He added briskly, "As for the herald, I know just the man, a voice like a bull horn, always ready to gamble for high stakes. And that's what we're doing—a gamble for the highest stakes of all, a gamble we have to take."

"When will you go?" said Hezekiah at last.

"We must be quick," said Amos. Taharka smiled as once again, perhaps for the last time, he repeated the old refrain: "There is no time."

And on the following morning they stood together in the chariot of the ambassador, the driver and herald in the front, and Amos whispered:

"You said once you were chosen by mistake. We in Judah believe that our God does not make mistakes. Let's find out."

25

The Confrontation

THE BLACK tents circled the many-colored tabernacle. After the great swarm of Sennacherib's camp, after the endless lines of horses, the rows of the terrible rammed towers, they seemed few and paltry, only the tabernacle itself rivaling the proud tent of the Assyrian king.

And there was another difference.

This was a defeated army.

The soldiers sat by their cook pots, heads hanging down, little heart left in them for talk and games. Even the rumor of news had awakened little interest. Would the king of Judah offer tribute to Pharaoh? What would *they* get out of it? The ostrich plumes drooped. The standards of the tribes, with their beasts' heads, hung limp. Beyond them lay the tents for the wounded, and Taharka remembered the school for the children of the god and the lessons in anatomy.

How many of them had died?

His eyes were drawn again to the tabernacle.

He was in there.

He was very angry, Taharka knew. Shabataka didn't like to lose. But he had been given a second chance. He would go back to Thebes, to Napata, with a victory after all. Like Rameses the Great he, too, would have tribute from the land of Canaan.

And Taharka knew he would make them pay dearly for the humiliation he had suffered.

A line of the tall Somali soldiers barred the approach to the tabernacle. Amos' voice was in his ear.

"Say nothing. You are the king. I will speak for you."

The voice of the Judahite herald, the voice like a bull horn, shivered the air.

"A message from my king for him who calls himself king of Kush and Pharaoh of Egypt."

For the first time there was a stir among the soldiers.

Who *calls* himself?

What was this?

A man came from the tabernacle. Another spokesman. Another "Rab Shaka." Taharka didn't recognize him. He, too, was a Somali.

"Let them pass. Let the messengers of Judah approach the chair of Pharaoh."

The herald looked at Taharka and Amos. Amos shook his head.

"Let him who calls himself Pharaoh come out."

The Somali spokesman returned to the tent. For just a moment he had looked hard at Taharka, surprised and curious.

Let *him* be curious too, Taharka prayed in silence
—to Horus the Hawk or Jahveh of the Mountain,
he didn't know which. Let him be curious enough to
come out. Let him come!

The flap of the tent was drawn back.

The god came forth.

A god, indeed, cloaked in the leopard skin, the
double crown upon his head. Taharka was back again
in the children's court in Napata as the god his father passed by. He wanted to fall on his knees and
shield his eyes with the soldiers, he feared that the
radiance might blind him—

But his eyes held. As on that day on the docks at
Thebes, he stood erect. And as on that day on the
docks at Thebes, he saw Shabataka's eyes widen in
recognition.

Amos was speaking.

"Will you hear our message, Shabataka prince of
Kush?"

"On your knees!" shouted the Somali spokesman.
"On your knees before the god!"

"What god?" cried Amos. "I don't see a god. I see
a man waiting for news. Joyful news, Shabataka! Your
brother has been restored to you. Taharka, king and
Pharaoh, has been restored to his people!"

Taharka?

For a moment the silence hung in the air, like
something a man could feel.

Then the whispers began, then the voices, rising
in the air like a wind.

Taharka?

The people, Talos had said, were not really stupid. And these *were* the people—the men of Kush, farmers and laborers and herders of cattle, chosen by lot, two out of every ten. They had wondered, never daring to speak. What had really become of Pharaoh —the kindly boy who had softened the priests' judgments—who, it was said, had once run over to pick up an old lady's comb for her? How had he died? At whose command?

Had he died at all?

They had been forbidden to say his name. But suddenly that name was on every tongue.

Taharka? Taharka? Taharka alive?

Shabataka's eyes had never left his brother's. On that day on the docks at Thebes he had been taken by surprise, not yet sure of his course. But now, with that forbidden name rising all around him, he knew he had no choice. He knew he had no time.

"Strike them down."

The Somali guards lifted their swords and moved forward.

Taharka closed his eyes, then opened them. A king must die bravely. The Somali guards did not seem to be in a hurry. And Amos, always watchful, saw that there were those among the other men who had risen from their knees, who had moved closer to the young Kushite in the shepherd's cloak, whose hands were feeling for their weapons.

Shabataka could see it too. Hesitation. A god could

not allow hesitation. He must have obedience, instant obedience, or he was no longer a god.

And if he were not a god—

"Strike them down!"

Taharka looked at him sharply. There was something in that voice, that voice from his childhood. Something he had never heard in it before. Uncertainty. Or was it fear?

There was a question in every mind, a question too terrible to be asked, much less answered.

"Taharka, king and Pharaoh, has been restored to his people."

Were they, for the first time ever, looking upon the face of the god? Frightened, some of them had hidden their eyes.

But the Somali guards had been well trained. They had always been proud of the son of their princess. They had been given a command. But before they could reach the chariot, a man stepped out from among the throng.

"It's him."

He didn't have a powerful voice, but in that silence it could be clearly heard.

"It's him. It's Taharka. I know him. I have seen his face."

And Taharka had seen *his* face, heard his voice. Where? When?

A long time ago. The river. The green banks of Kush, the black mud and the hot, hot sun—

"He took his spear and killed the beast that would

have killed me. And then he took his sacred cloth and
tied up my wound and kept the life inside me. Just
like a doctor. But he's not. He's Taharka. He's the
God."

The man got down on his knees. He bent his face
to the earth.

There was a harsh cry from the blue sky above. A
swiftly falling shadow. A hawk, for whom Taharka
had been named. It flapped down, and came to rest
on Taharka's wrist. It screamed again, and flew suddenly straight at Shabataka.

Shabataka ducked. The bird passed over his head.

"A sign! The Hawk has spoken!" A tall black soldier, in the regalia of a commander, had come to the
fore of the crowd. "Remember the other portents!
The Sun himself has told us that we are led by no
true Pharaoh!"

There was a strange sound, a stirring and shuffling,
the low hum of voices.

Soldiers were falling to their knees, shielding their
faces, whispering the unbelievable words.

"Taharka. Pharaoh. Taharka. King of Kush."

"Strike them down!" It was Shabataka, almost
screaming now.

And the voice of Amos: "Jahveh be praised. We've
won!"

It was true. A small group of Kushites had fallen
upon the Somali bodyguard and driven them back.
Shabataka was surrounded.

For the first time, Taharka spoke, crying out over the confusion:

"Do not touch him! Put up your swords! Bring him to his tent."

⊌ 26 ⊌

The Return of a King

THE TWO brothers stood face to face in the tent of the king. Kushite guards stood by the entrance. Outside could be heard the voice of the herald, crying endlessly: "Taharka, Son of the Sun, Child of the Hawk, Lord of Kush, Great God of Napata and Meroe, Pharaoh of Egypt—he has returned!"

"So, Pharaoh has returned!" said Shabataka. "Well, Hari? What will it be? The strangler's rope? The fire? The stake?"

Taharka closed his eyes.

"Embutah. You killed him. You tried to kill me."

"Him, yes. He made me crawl. You, no. Not before today." He smiled suddenly. "A funny thing—I liked you. At first I even tried to help you."

And he had. Takarka remembered: No, no, no! That's *not* what I meant—You don't obey the sun priest, he obeys you!

"But I know now I would have killed you. Sooner or later. It would have had to be done."

Not before today. The taster. That first sly, evil

202

attempt. It *had* been the Assyrians. For some reason
Taharka was glad.

And suddenly he knew what he was going to do.
His eyes were as hard and sure as his brother's. He
motioned to the soldiers.

Shabataka was again surrounded. He watched his
brother, still smiling.

"The robe," said Taharka.

Shabataka's smile faded. Slowly he slid the leopard
skin from his shoulders. He threw it to his brother.

"The gold," said Taharka.

They fell in a clanking heap at Shabataka's feet—
the rings, the arm bands, the collar of gold.

"The crown of the Two Lands."

He took it from his brother's hands. He looked at
it for a moment. It was his now: by his own choice,
the choice of the army—and the choice of the gods.
Taharka set it upon his head.

He held out his shepherd's cloak.

"Put it on."

Then, to the commander of the soldiers, the man
who had spoken to the people: "Appoint trusted men.
Send him under guard in all secrecy to the land of
the Somalis. There give him money and food and set
him free."

Forgive me, Embutah. He's my brother. Besides,
he owed the God of Amos an act of mercy—he
who had been spared with the people of Jerusalem.

And to Shabataka, "If ever again you cross into
Nile country, your life is forfeit."

Taharka was not a fool.

Neither was Shabataka. His brother was the army's choice. Who of his mother's tribesmen could stand against Egypt? It was over. At that moment he would have preferred the sentence of death.

One last time he spoke to the son of his father. "You begin to sound like a king, my brother. Maybe someday you will learn to be one." One last time he was the experienced older brother in the garden with the lotus pool. "You had better learn quickly. They'll be back, you know. The Assyrians. Maybe not too soon. But they'll be back."

Impatient now, the guards thrust him out into the open. Taharka could no longer see his face.

For the last time, he heard his voice. "Use the time you have, little brother. Use it well."

Taharka stood in Pharaoh's royal chariot, the leopard skin hanging from his shoulders.

He would ride through the camp, would be proclaimed God-King of the Two Lands. Soon he would be back in Thebes.

Yes, Shepnuset, I will return.

There would be times, through the years, when they would be together. He was the god and she was the priestess. They would manage that.

Shabataka. He would not have them cut out his name from the statues. He would not remove it from the books of the priests. After all, he himself had not really been king until today—today, when he had chosen and been chosen. He would let his brother have his due.

Amos stood by the chariot. He motioned to the herald.

"Ride with Pharaoh through the camp. Proclaim the true king."

Taharka held out his hand.

"Amos. Come."

But Amos shook his head. This was the chariot of the king. Amos was withdrawing from him. With head bowed, the envoy from Judah stood before the king of Egypt and Kush. He would never come to him again as a friend, only as an ambassador to a king.

Then, as the charioteer gathered up the reins, he raised his head and smiled. And Taharka knew that Amos would remember, remember the curtain rope, and Hezekiah's tunnel, how they had stood together against the Assyrians. Whether or not they ever met again, they would always be friends. Taharka reached out his arm. Their hands came together in one strong fist. Then the chariot moved out.

"Behold Taharka, Son of the Sun, Child of the Hawk, Lord of Kush, Great God of Napata and Meroe, Pharaoh of Egypt—"

Endlessly, throughout the camp.

Once Taharka smiled, almost laughed. On the outskirts of the encampment were the tents of the Mucri. They had followed the Kushites, hoping for a chance at the Assyrians, a chance to avenge their tribe.

They're like Amos, thought Taharka. They never give up.

"Taharka, Son of the Sun, Child of the Hawk, Lord of Kush—"

"Haru!"

A little boy had ridden out from the Mucri camp on a silver gray donkey.

"Stop," said Taharka to the charioteer.

The little boy rode up close. He looked earnestly into the face of the god. He even rested his hand on the wheel of the sacred chariot.

On this strange day, the soldiers were hardly surprised.

"Are you really a king, Haru?"

Taharka nodded.

"I knew it. I always knew you were a prince."

"You're a prince, too, Sabi. Someday you'll be a chief." He'll be a good chief, he thought. He'll be a good man.

"Take good care of Hermes."

"I know. And never let him serve the Assyrians."

"And Sabi—"

The horses were prancing, restless to be on their way. Taharka called back to the boy on the donkey. "Be kind to the stranger who comes to your well. Who knows? He might be a king!"

Author's Note

TAHARKA used his time well. He held the two lands together and, by the time of the great Assyrian invasion several years after this story, Egypt was strong enough to hold them off at the border. Sennacherib's son, Esarhaddon, died in a second attempt at conquest. Twenty years later, near death, Taharka halted them again, outside Thebes, and drove them back down the Nile. For the next thirty years, under his successors, the deadlock continued, exhausting the strength of the Assyrian empire and leading to its final collapse.

The few records we have for this time often contradict each other. There are no precise dates and the Assyrians' chronicle says that old Shabaka was king during the siege of Jerusalem. The Bible says it was Taharka ("Tirhakah, king of Ethiopia" II Kings 19:9) and this book follows the Biblical version. The Assyrians also boast of the later destruction of Thebes, but we know that Thebes was thriving and successfully carrying on the struggle until the dissolution of the Assyrian empire.

Little is recorded of Taharka beyond the fact that he overcame the Pharaoh Shabataka in a struggle for the crown of the Nile and was the first king of Egypt to fight the Assyrians. There is no information on his maternal parentage. But throughout history slave soldiers like Embutah have risen to the highest positions in African and Middle Eastern armies, and their kings (including the sultans of Morocco and Oman) have sometimes been the sons of southern African slave women, as Taharka is in my story.

Shabataka appears in the king lists before Taharka. But a later legend suggests a savage bitterness in the contest for the double crown (Shabataka burned alive!) and it is very probable that Taharka was reclaiming what had been taken from him. Taharka's generosity (on which I based my character and which contradicts the legend) is suggested by the fact that, unlike most Pharoahs, he never erased his rival's name from the lists of kings.

The Bible tells the story of the "smiting of the Assyrians" before the wall of Jerusalem and the sign of the retreating sun in three places: in II Kings, chapters 18 though 21, and also in II Chronicles chapter 32 and Isaiah chapter 36. It is not clear from the Biblical account what exactly happened to the besieging army, but it is certain a great many soldiers died very suddenly. The Greek historian Herodotus says an army of mice chewed the points off the Assyrian spears. In this book it is suggested that the disaster may have been caused by a swift-acting form of bubonic plague. Sennacherib, when he wrote the stories of his exploits, boasted that he had "shut up the King of Israel like a bird in a cage." He does not claim, however, to have conquered Jerusalem.

King Hezekiah was able to withstand the siege partly because of his foresight in digging a tunnel from the spring outside the city into the pool of Siloam. Today, if you visit Jerusalem, you can wade down the same channel that helped save the lives of the Israelites over twenty-five hundred years ago.

HEZEKIAH'S
TUNNEL

About the Author

JOANNE S. WILLIAMSON was born in 1926, in Arlington, Massachusetts. Though she had interests in both writing and music, and attended Barnard College and Diller Quaile School of Music, it was writing which became the primary focus for her career after college. She was a feature writer for Connecticut newspapers until 1965, when she moved to Kennebunkport, Maine and began to write historical fiction for young people.

In each of Miss Williamson's novels, now totaling eight with *God King*, she explores unusual historical slants of well-known events. In her first book, *Jacobins Daughter*, she tells a true story of the French Revolution; in *The Eagles Have Flown*, she presents a picture of Julius Caesar's time and gives a sympathetic portrayal of Brutus. She has a remarkable knack for using her fictional characters and plot to make connections between real historical persons and events. In a time when history is often taught in bits and pieces these connections are a great help, not only to the younger reader, but to the older one as well. Her third book, *Hittite Warrior*, has been well received in its recent reprinting for just this facility in showing the inter-relatedness of the ancient Hittite, Hebrew, Canaanite and Greek peoples in the 12th century before Christ. In *God King,* written some years ago, but now published for the first time, similar fascinating connections are made for a later period in Israel's history.

Of *God King,* Miss Williamson says, "I first came across a king called Taharka ('King of Ethiopia and Egypt') in the Bible's story of King Hezekiah and the saving of Jerusalem from the Assyrians. Never having heard of him, I was curious. I looked through the histories of Egypt and found what I could—very little! There were, however, old legends (including the rivalry with his brother), Assyrian annals and, best of all, anthropological studies of Africa south of Egypt. What I found gave a picture of a remarkable character, a Kushite (Sudanese) king of Egypt who stood against the Assyrians and halted their advance through the civilized world. The Assyrian annals contradicted this, but the physical evidence contradicts them. I found myself caught up in a fascinating might-have-been story and decided to tell it."

Before *God King* (and the reprinting of *Hittite Warrior*), Joanne Williamson's last book to be published had been *To Dream Upon a Crown* in 1967. The issue of this retelling of Shakespeare's Henry VI trilogy coincided with the unfortunate decline in America of interest in intelligent historical fiction for young people. At that time, she returned to her second calling and taught music until her retirement in 1990. Now interest has been rekindled in her books and in those of other writers of historical fiction. This renewal should be a great source of satisfaction to the many readers, young and old, who are discovering again the fascination of man's story throughout the ages.

Joanne Williamson died July 5, 2002.